THE GIRL WITH FLAMING HAIR

Natalie Kleinman

SAPERE
BOOKS

THE GIRL WITH FLAMING HAIR

Published by Sapere Books.

20 Windermere Drive, Leeds, England, LS17 7UZ,
United Kingdom

saperebooks.com

ISBN: 978-1-80055-299-9

In memory of my mother, Debbie
The feistiest heroine of them all
Always in my heart

CHAPTER ONE

Rufus Solgrave was whistling to himself as he tooled his carriage down the lane. Behind him was his country seat and ahead of him the expectation of a week of pleasure in the shires. Though the summer of 1818 had been uncomfortably hot, autumn had brought a pleasant cooling which bode well for the activities to come. He went at the invitation of his friend, Oliver Bridlington, with the added promise that he would be mounted in style and need not bring his own horses. Thus, he was travelling in relative comfort with the intention of completing his journey in stages and the anticipation of hugely enjoying the experience. What he did not expect was the necessity of pulling up his team because a grey mare was standing rider-less at the edge of the road.

"Jump down, if you would, Wilfred, and see if you can't catch the bridle," he said to his groom as he stopped short, not wanting to risk scaring what he could see was a lady's horse, for it carried a side-saddle. "No, wait. Hold their heads. I'll go myself."

He approached quietly, uttering soothing sounds, and realised soon enough that the mare wasn't going anywhere. She was standing guard over a woman lying on the grass verge. Rufus quickened his pace and dropped to his knees beside the inert figure. He was grateful to find a weak pulse at her wrist but, though he could see no obvious sign of injury, she was out cold. Wasting no time, he lifted her and carried her back to the carriage. The horse followed, nudging him as she did so.

"Don't worry, girl. I'll look after your mistress. You deserve an apple for not making a bolt for your stable, and I shall see you get one shortly. But first we must take the lady back to Ashby and get the doctor to examine her."

At a raised eyebrow from his master, the grin was wiped from Wilfred's face. It wasn't the first time he'd heard Lord Luxton addressing a horse. Rather fond of them, he was. Laying his burden in the carriage, Rufus flung off his many-caped coat to reveal a fine figure of a man, whose long legs were encased in tight breeches and whose well-cut jacket could not hide the muscles beneath. Throwing the outer garment over the young woman, he could see curls of the most vibrant red escaping in wisps from the confines of her green bonnet, a perfect match for a riding habit which had become sadly streaked with stains during the accident. Returning to the horses' heads, he asked Wilfred to hold the mare while he manoeuvred the conveyance to face back the way he had come.

"It would seem, Wilfred, that our excursion will be delayed, at least for today. We must return home for the time being. Jump up."

Cursing the limitations of a carriage that was not designed to carry passengers, Rufus propped the lady in a seated position beside him. Putting his left arm around her to prevent a fall, he promised to apologise later. Her head fell against his shoulder, and he could discern a scent which he was unable to identify but which pleased him. He smiled, took up the reins in his other hand, and was smiling still as, one-handed but with the ease of an expert, he turned his curricle into the gates at the head of the drive which led to Ashby. A footman came out to greet him and he gave orders for the doctor to be summoned immediately. Then, leaving Wilfred to take charge of the horses and carriage, he picked up his unconscious burden and carried her into the house.

"The door, if you please," Rufus said, addressing a second footman and nodding towards the drawing room. It was opened and he entered, to the surprise of his mother and his sister, Lydia, who were both engrossed in studying dress patterns and had not heard him arrive. As they jumped to their feet, he laid the invalid on a settee and once more checked her pulse. Still faint, but, as far as he could tell, no worse.

"What has happened, Rufus? How do you come to be carrying Miss Clifford? Why is she hurt? Are you injured? We must send for the doctor."

"Don't distress yourself, Mama. I have already summoned Bolton and hope he will be here soon. I am relieved that you are acquainted with the lady, for I had no clue as to who she might be. I found her lying by the road, some short distance from home. Not knowing where to take her, I brought her here, so I am afraid you must put up with me for at least one more day," he said, with no little regret.

"Lydia, where are my smelling salts?" his mother demanded. Lydia placed them under Miss Clifford's nose. They were of no avail. Her breathing was shallow, but she stirred not at all. Rufus excused himself to change his attire but went first to the stable to give the promised titbit to the grey mare. She had been safely installed and her tack removed. There was no sign of distress and he complimented her on her temperament as, with good manners, she accepted the proffered apple.

"It seems you are to remain here for a while," he said, standing at her shoulder. She leaned in, giving him to understand that if this was how she was to be treated, she had no objection. "I shall endeavour to find out your name. In the meantime, I fear I must leave you and return to the house, but do not worry. Wilfred will see to your comfort, won't you,

Wilfred?" Rufus exited the stall, aware that his groom was standing by and grinning once more.

The earl went directly to his apartment and changed into pantaloons and a tailored blue jacket. He wore his mid-brown hair Brutus fashion and merely ran his fingers through it before joining the countess and Lydia in the drawing room. By this time, the doctor had arrived and was examining the patient.

"Thank you for attending so quickly, Doctor Bolton," Rufus said with the smile that endeared him to so many. "I'm afraid I was at a loss as to what to do. I hope I haven't caused added discomfort to the lady."

"None, I am happy to say, for nothing appears to be broken. However, it is my opinion that Miss Clifford is suffering from severe concussion and will no doubt have quite a headache when she awakes. I cannot judge when that will be and would suggest that she be removed to a bedchamber until such time as consciousness returns. Though I stand firm by my opinion that you will have done her no harm, I would strongly advise that she remain here. She is most certainly in no fit state to travel further. I will call again tomorrow to see how she goes on. Good day to you, sir. Lady Luxton. Miss Solgrave."

Rufus rang the bell and asked that the room his mother had designated be made ready for Miss Clifford and that he be informed when it was so, in order that he might carry her there. "And perhaps, Mama, we might send for her abigail. There is daylight enough still for her to reach here before nightfall, and it will relieve your own maid of the burden of looking after her when she begins to recover."

"I will write a note immediately, telling her family she is here and requesting that they do not call for the time being," his mother replied, adding with the mischievous smile her son had inherited, "I shall perhaps bend the truth a little by saying the doctor thought it inadvisable for her to receive visitors at this stage. Her father is a dreadful man, and as for the stepmother, well, I dare say you've met her sort before. I don't believe she and Sophie rub along well together. Not at all."

"No, I have it from Sophie herself, for she is my particular friend, even though we are not of an age," her daughter said, looking up in the act of removing their patient's bonnet.

"How is it, then, that I have never met her?"

His mother took the opportunity to remind him that his visits home were infrequent and that, as Lydia had not yet come out, such parties as they held at Ashby were informal and consisted only of those local people in whom she dared suggest her son would have no interest.

"You malign me, Mama. I hope I am not so puffed up in my own consequence that I cannot enjoy the company of others." But he was smiling, though his smile turned to wonder when, for the first time, he was able properly to see Sophie's face. Freed from restraint, her red curls now tumbled all around her. He thought he had never seen a more beautiful girl. While his mother scribbled a hasty but well-judged note and Lydia went to charge her own maid with finding a suitable nightgown for their visitor, Rufus had ample opportunity to study Sophie's countenance. A milky complexion was without blemish but any blush that might have been present had faded from her cheeks, no doubt due to the accident. Her cheekbones were high and her chin, he judged, was firm even in repose. Her eyes he could not see, for they were shadowed by lids which boasted thick lashes a shade darker than her hair. He was pulled from his abstraction when Lydia re-entered the room and announced that the bedchamber was ready. For the third time Rufus gathered the beauty in his arms and carried her upstairs. Once he had laid her upon the bed he departed, leaving his sister with the task of making her as comfortable as possible.

He joined his mother once more and sat to await the arrival of the abigail who was to bring some of the necessities the countess deemed essential during Sophie's period of recovery.

"I hope you are not too disappointed at the delay. I am aware how keenly you were anticipating joining the hunt."

"Not at all, Mama," he said, not entirely truthfully. "One day will make little difference and I doubt I can be of any assistance here, so I shall once more take my leave in the morning."

Lady Luxton was a shrewd woman and had never made any attempt to keep her son by her side. Nor did she do so now. His visits home were always a pleasure, for he came out of fondness rather than duty. His relationship with his sister was one of strong affection on both sides, despite the difference in their ages. But, being nine and twenty years old, there were other pursuits that called him away. His easy-going manner had earned him a large circle of friends and Oliver Bridlington, whom he had met while serving in the army, was the closest of these. Having sold his commission upon coming into the title at the death of his father, he could be found at most times expending his seemingly boundless energies on those occupations which best suited a man of wealth and ton. Army life had suited him well and it irked him to be still for long. When in London he might be found at Jackson's boxing saloon in Bond Street, or at one of his clubs. His fondness for horses would take him to Newmarket or Ascot and he lost no opportunity to indulge in any sporting activity he could find, though he had never been drawn in to some of the extremes that had proved to be the downfall of many a young buck.

"I trust Miss Clifford has sustained no serious injury, Rufus. The doctor seemed quite positive, don't you think?"

"How well I remember old Bolton's assurances when I suffered any childhood ailment. He was ever quick to assert that I would feel better in no time at all, and for the most part he was right. I have complete confidence in him or I would not leave tomorrow, for the responsibility is mine, not yours."

"What nonsense you talk sometimes, my son. We are all of us responsible for the welfare of our friends and neighbours to some degree. It was lucky you found Sophie and brought her here, but I am happy enough to have her in my care. You could hardly have left her lying at the side of the road, after all."

They chatted amiably until a gig arrived carrying the maid and the luggage she had brought with her. Both Rufus and his mother were relieved that Sophie's family had taken heed of their request not to visit, though Lady Luxton was not at all surprised that they would so readily abnegate any perceived duty. The maid was escorted to her mistress's room and Lydia, who had been sitting with her friend lest she stir, joined her mother, while her brother went to inform his staff that he would be leaving straight after breakfast and they should have all in readiness. The three of them dined in the small dining room, foregoing the grandeur of the larger apartment that was kept for more formal occasions.

Rufus left the next day after taking leave of his parent and expressing the hope that she would not be too burdened by the obligation which had now fallen upon her.

"What a rogue you are when I know well that you cannot wait to be gone. Do pay my respects to young Bridlington and write to me of your success in the field."

"I will, Mama, I promise," he replied, and his mama stood and watched the carriage travel out of sight before returning to the house to see if there had been any overnight change in her guest. An hour later, Doctor Bolton arrived.

The countess had retired to the drawing room while the doctor carried out his examination, leaving her daughter to escort him downstairs when he was ready. She was confident of a happy outcome but could not rest easily until they joined her. She was concerned to see a small furrow between the doctor's eyes.

"There is no sign yet of a return to consciousness, Lady Luxton, and I fear the concussion is deeper than I had first supposed. I do not despair, though. I can see no evidence of a contusion. There are no bumps or swellings. No breaking of the skin. I feel certain that Lord Luxton would have mentioned it, had he seen a boulder or some such thing."

"I am afraid he left the county earlier this morning so we are unable to ask him, but I believe he said he'd found her by a large oak tree. Perhaps she knocked her head on an overhanging branch which caused her to be unseated. Might that have been the cause, do you think?"

"It's possible, of course. We can only speculate. We must be grateful she was wearing a riding hat which must, I am sure, have afforded her some protection. Miss Clifford's pulse is steady and, I think, a little stronger today. I am a great believer that the body heals itself." He smiled and added, "Perhaps I should not say so, for what further need would you have of me if that were always the case? However, it is sometimes so and I am convinced that, given time, our patient will make a full recovery. I shall come again tomorrow. Good day, ladies."

"Good day, doctor, and thank you. Lydia, perhaps you could ring for the footman to show Doctor Bolton to the door."

"No need, madam. Do not disturb yourself, Miss Solgrave. I know the way."

Lydia was sitting next to the bed reading when Sophie began to stir. Sophie awoke with no idea where she was other than that she was neither in her own bed nor in her own room. In addition, she had a headache the like of which she had never before experienced. Her moaning brought Lydia to her side immediately.

"It's all right, Sophie. You've had a fall. My brother found you and brought you back here to Ashby."

Her friend was evidently confused, and it took a moment or two for her to get her bearings.

"But… Why? Snowflake! I remember. I was riding. I fell. Is she … ow!" Sophie had tried to sit up, but her head began to swim and she sank back once more against the pillows.

"Snowflake is fine and is stabled here, so you'll be able to visit her as soon as you are well enough. In the meantime, you must rest. The doctor has promised to return tomorrow to see how you go on. I'll just fetch Mama. We have all been anxious about you and she will want to know you are awake."

When she returned some minutes later carrying a jug of lemonade, Lydia found that her patient had once more fallen asleep but there was now a tinge of natural colour in her cheeks. Setting the jug down on a small table, she turned and raised a finger to her lips so that her mother, who was right behind her, would come no further.

"Let us not wake her, Mama. Her abigail will call if she stirs again."

Their greatest concern had been alleviated, for Sophie, once she had assimilated her surroundings, had been quite coherent when she woke. Lady Luxton wrote another note to her family, still adjuring them not to come but reassuring them that Miss Clifford had returned to consciousness and was now sleeping peacefully. Lydia went to the hothouse to cut some blooms for her friend and returned to find the jug half empty.

"She woke all of a sudden, miss. That thirsty, she was, she drank two glasses with barely a pause before going off again, like."

"Thank you, Bertha. I will sit with her if you'd like to stretch your legs. Go to the kitchen and cook will give you something to eat. Come back when you are ready. I'm happy to remain for a while, and tonight you may sleep once more on the truckle bed behind the screen. I wouldn't want Miss Clifford to wake and find herself alone."

"Oh no, miss, I wouldn't rightly like to leave her."

"Very well, off you go, then," Lydia insisted, as poor Bertha lingered. She settled down with her book but, aware of a change, she looked up to find Sophie open-eyed and smiling at her.

"You're feeling better, I hope. Is there anything I can get you?"

"No, I thank you, for you have brought sunshine into the room with these beautiful flowers. And I had a dreadful headache, but that is easing now. I think I might be able to sleep again, but perhaps some more of your delicious lemonade first, if you don't mind."

"I'm delighted you are enjoying it, for I made it myself and will make some more. Bertha will be back to stay with you shortly, and I'll see you in the morning. Sleep is the best thing for you now, my friend. I feel certain you will be up and about again in no time."

CHAPTER TWO

After an uneventful journey, Lord Luxton arrived in Leicestershire to a warm welcome from Oliver Bridlington, who came out to meet him.

"Glad you could make it, old boy. We've had some great sport this week. Bagged quite a few today. Come in. Come in," he said, wringing his friend's hand.

Rufus laughed and followed his host into a house of quite expansive proportions in which, as ever, he felt immediately at ease. How much might be attributed to its jovial owner and how much to its configuration he could not say, but a roaring fire and a room full of men, with most of whom he was already acquainted, set the pattern for the days to come. A glass was placed in his hand and, when he protested that he must change his clothing after a day on the road, it was pointed out to him that all would shortly be adjourning to dress for dinner and it was unnecessary to go through the exercise twice.

"In any case," said Freddie Conroy, another friend from his army days, "you would be wasting good drinking time. Ollie has a fine cellar here, you know."

"Which no doubt you will attempt to work your way through in one visit, eh, Freddie?" Rufus said, to the amusement of the assembled company. "But if you're happy to excuse my dirt, I am happy to do whatever I can to aid you."

He was surprised when, a little while later, a note was brought to him from his groom. When his master joined him in the hall, the lad said, "I thought you might be wishful of seeing this straight away. Wedged in a corner it was, and I only found it cos I was giving the carriage a good going over after a couple of days on the road."

Nestled in the palm of his hand was a locket which Rufus had never seen before. It belonged neither to his mother nor his sister. Then he remembered the young lady — what was her name? Ah yes, Miss Clifford. Doubtless it belonged to her. He opened the locket, but the face it portrayed meant nothing to him.

"Thank you, Wilfred. You did right to bring it to me." He then placed it in his pocket and forgot about it immediately. However, when he went later to his room, his valet, having aided him in removing his coat, found it reposing where it had been left and, holding it up, shot a look of reproof at the earl.

"Yes, I know, Bixby. You take it as a personal affront but, believe me, I had nowhere else to put it at the time." The smile that won such loyalty from all his staff had no apparent effect on this gentleman's gentleman, but no further rebuke was forthcoming and Rufus knew he'd been forgiven. "Lay it on the dresser, if you please. I shall decide later what to do with it. In the meantime, we must hurry or I shall be late for supper."

The word 'hurry' was loosely interpreted, as neither man would forego whatever might be necessary to turn out Lord Luxton in sartorial splendour. The earl was not a vain man but neither was he indifferent to his appearance. Having served in the army and proud to have worn its uniform, he continued afterwards to invest time to ensure he was as well turned out as he could be. When Bixby let go his breath after his master's fifth attempt with a cravat proved successful, he aided him into his coat and stood back to survey his work. He saw a specimen of manliness whose fine legs were encased in dove-grey pantaloons and whose coat was the colour of the midnight sky. The cravat was arranged in a style of Luxton's own design and set off with a diamond pin. He wore only a single signet ring besides and the whole was a perfect study in simplicity. Grateful that he was fortunate enough to serve such a well-proportioned individual, able to do justice to the efforts of an expert, Bixby was satisfied.

There was no formality at the meal, which was attended by six men, all talking at once and across the table. It was as they sat drinking port, the covers having been removed, that Rufus recounted the reason for his delay in joining them. "A beautiful young woman as good as fell into my arms," he said, smiling broadly. "And with no clue as to who she was, what else could I do but return with her to Ashby? I can only be grateful that my mother knew Miss Clifford, or I might still be detained at home. There was temptation, of course. I have never seen her equal, but, gentlemen, I was promised to you. And the lure of the hunt was the greater."

They all laughed, one confessing he would probably have chosen the beautiful woman over the hunt and another asking, "Clifford, you say? Which county did you say you come from?"

"Buckinghamshire. Why?"

"Well, if it's the family I'm thinking of, there's something very rum about them."

"Indeed?"

"I don't like to gossip," Pontonby said mendaciously, "but there was talk that the girl was no kin of Clifford. The mother died in childbirth, I believe, after some havey-cavey goings-on outside of the marriage."

"But if the child wasn't his, why would he raise her as his own?" Ollie put in.

"To save face, no doubt. Nothing was proved, but you know how these things get about."

"Well, my groom has found her locket in my carriage. As I don't know when I shall next return home, I must be sure and send it to her. It holds the likeness of a young woman whom I must assume to be her mother, and no doubt she will be distressed when she finds it missing."

Ollie pushed his chair back from the table and said, "Time to adjourn, I think. Anyone for a game of cards?"

A lover of all physical sports, Rufus was not enamoured of the card table and chose instead to stand by the fire, one elbow resting on the mantelpiece. The noise of the rest receded into the background as the image of a beautiful girl with glorious red hair and a milky complexion swam before his eyes.

CHAPTER THREE

By the time Sophie received her locket, she was well on the road to recovery. Lady Luxton could give her no clear idea of her son's movements, so the best she could do was write to him at his London home to thank him for all he had done for her. Her progress had been rapid but she showed no inclination to return to Charnwood, having been assured by her hostess that she might remain for as long as she liked.

"I have been a charge on you for long enough, Lady Luxton. I do not like to be seen imposing on your good nature."

"Nonsense, and I wish you will call me Elizabeth, for it makes me feel quite old to be addressed all the time as Lady Luxton. I'm sure we are well enough acquainted now to be on first name terms. Anyway," she added, "you are company for Lydia and, as I am contemplating taking her to London before too long, I make no doubt there is much you could tell her, for she is looking forward to her come-out with as much trepidation as excitement."

"I fear I can be of little help in that regard, La— Elizabeth. Mama did not see fit to take me to London. I have never been outside the confines of Buckinghamshire." Though she spoke in a cheery manner, there was no hiding the regret that lay behind these words.

"But that's outrageous!"

"She could not, she said, leave my father for such an extended period. She has always maintained that he is not a hale man, and he never ventures far from home. In my opinion, however, I believe that she cossets him excessively, for I've never in my life seen him suffer a day's illness. I am content enough, though, for I am lucky to have many friends in the neighbourhood, of which you are well aware as we have met often at other houses. I do not lack for companionship or entertainment."

Lady Luxton opened her mouth to speak but thought better of it. It wasn't for her to disparage the baron and Lady Clifford to their daughter. Instead she sought a solution and found one within moments.

"Would your parents have any objection, do you think, if I begged them to allow you to extend your stay here and come with us when we go to London? It would be such a help to me, for you would be able to relieve me of some of the burden, you know. I'm not as young as I was, and there will be much to do in the way of shopping for clothes and organising parties and the like."

There was nothing in the slightest way frail about Elizabeth Solgrave and both knew it, but each seized upon this admirable excuse to put forward their case. Sophie was as sure as she could be that her mama would not approve, but she would also be hard put to raise any acceptable objection.

"With your permission, I shall write to them myself." A smile of pure mischief played around Sophie's mouth, and Elizabeth would have given much to have known what she was thinking. "I cannot thank you enough and, if all is agreed, I daresay I shall be as much filled with excitement and trepidation as Lydia is."

The response to Sophie's letter home was a visit the next day from her stepbrother, Francis Follet. A squarish man of medium height and with an insufferably haughty manner, he had bullied her almost from the moment of his mother's marriage to her father. She could not like him. As they had matured into adulthood, his bullying had been replaced with a patronising air that indicated he knew what was best for her. He had, in fact, on several occasions said as much. Sophie had been surprised, therefore, when his attitude towards her had, some two years previously, become lover-like and, though she had refused him more than once, he seemed to assume that she would ultimately become his wife. She was hardly astonished, then, when he was shown into her hostess's morning room with the obvious intention of turning her from her plan. Bowing as he entered, he said in the most ingratiating way, "My dear Lady Luxton, Miss Solgrave. My mother sends her compliments and asks me to thank you for your care of my sister."

Resisting the urge to giggle, Elizabeth acknowledged him with a slow nod, as unctuous as his own. "We are delighted to have her with us, and indeed I cannot imagine how I went on before she came. You have come, I am sure, to express your mother's obligation to me in person for inviting Miss Clifford to remain and journey with us to London in a month or so."

Sophie resorted to hiding her face in her handkerchief and Lydia turned her gaze to the window, biting firmly on her lower lip. This upstart was no match for Lady Luxton.

"Not at all, though we are, all of us, naturally flattered."

"Why on earth would you be so? It is Sophie we invite, not you. But I forget my manners. Do please sit down."

He was not proof against her direct look and instead seated himself next to his stepsister in what the rest all felt was a proprietorial manner.

"I know my sister better than you," he said, the awful smile once more apparent, "and I am convinced that her delightful manners leave her without the means to refuse your kind invitation."

"What rubbish you do talk, Francis. I have no intention of refusing. Lady Luxton is willing to allow me to join her party, and I have accepted gratefully. You cannot imagine how very happy I am at the prospect of seeing so many new things that have thus far been denied me."

"You cannot have thought, Sophie. Your circumstances are … unusual."

It was a term he had used to her in the past but now, as then, she had no idea what he was alluding to.

"Unusual in that I have all my life been confined to Buckinghamshire. You would not deny me this opportunity, surely?"

He was backed into a corner, but Follet was not a man who was easily swayed from his purpose. Elizabeth watched with amusement.

"You must see, my dear," he continued in a tone so patronising that Lydia's gaze was drawn to his face in disbelief, "that, given the understanding between us, I would not wish you to be indulging in all kinds of excesses that might be deemed unsuitable."

Lady Luxton felt it was time to intercede. "Excesses! Unsuitable! What on earth do you think I shall be asking your sister to undertake?"

The young man faltered for a moment but still would not be halted and, throwing caution to the wind, he said, "Perhaps you are unaware, my lady, that I hope to make Sophie my wife. There is an acknowledgement between us that it shall be so."

This was going too far, and his chosen bride said in an air as haughty as his own, "The acknowledgement is, I fear, only on your side, Francis. I have never given you reason to believe I would marry you. Far from it. Forgive me for mentioning this in front of others, but it was you who raised the subject. I have on several occasions rejected your kind offer and I would thank you not to renew it in the future. I will never be your wife. I think it is time you left. Do please convey my fondest wishes to our parents and tell them I shall write to them from town."

She stood, as did her companions, and Follet had little choice but to take his leave, saying sullenly as he went, "I hope you do not live to regret this day, for it will be hard to find another who is willing to take you."

Sophie stared after him with a puzzled look on her face and Lydia moved to comfort her. "Why on earth would he say anything so intolerable?" she asked.

"I do not know. He has insinuated as much before, but I have never been able to bring him to explain himself. No doubt he has manufactured something in his own mind to account for my rejection, for I know he believes himself to be perfection personified." It wasn't sufficient explanation but she had no other and, as on previous occasions, she resolved to put it out of her mind. "However, we have now negotiated that hurdle and they cannot prevent me from remaining with you, if you will still have me, Elizabeth. I am, after all, of age and may do as I please."

It was the truth, of course, but Francis's words had put a check on Sophie's enthusiasm and it took the combined efforts of Elizabeth and Lydia to coax her out of the dismals.

Within a few days any thoughts of being dismal were forgotten in a whirl of activity. While Lady Luxton had every intention of visiting dressmakers, milliners, haberdashers and any others who might turn her daughter out in style, she was equally determined that they should, none of them, visit London looking dowdy. She had an innate sense of fashion which her daughter had inherited. A period of indulgence ensued which all three ladies enjoyed to the utmost, local modistes falling over themselves to ensure that it was their name the noble lady carried with her to the capital. Sophie, a wealthy young woman in her own right, having inherited her fortune from her mother, had no need to suffer the embarrassment of being her hostess's pensioner. Indeed, Elizabeth was convinced that it was on account of her affluence that Follet was pursuing her. She was sure of it when he came two days after his previous visit to apologise for his hasty comments, and he was at his most ingratiating. Sophie was fortunate enough to be absent as she was out riding with Lydia, a daily activity which was enjoyed equally by both. Sadly, Sophie's riding habit had not recovered from the fall as well as she. A replacement had been ordered, once more in her favourite green, but for the time being the other was still serviceable, though it would not do if she were to ride in London. As for Follet, the countess sent him off with a flea in his ear and derived a great deal of pleasure recounting the incident when the others returned.

"I cannot credit that he didn't insist on remaining to speak to me in person," Sophie said as she laughed and thanked her hostess for disposing of this thorn in her side.

"Oh believe me, he tried, my dear, but I have dealt with better men than he in the past. I cannot be sure but I think he was mumbling under his breath as he left. I am certain he will not bother you again before we leave."

Lydia hugged her mother in appreciation. "I would back you against anyone, Mama. Poor man. I almost feel sorry for him."

"Oh no, don't. You haven't seen him at his worst. I should not speak so in front of you, Elizabeth, but Lydia knows that things do not stand well for me at home. Being here with you has been for me like a breath of fresh air."

"And so I should hope," laughed Lydia. "Anything would be after being compelled to spend time with Francis Follet."

All that remained was for Elizabeth to write to her son and inform him that she would be taking up residence for an extended period in the house in Grosvenor Square, to which address she directed her letter in the hope he might be at home.

CHAPTER FOUR

Rufus, who had indeed returned to Grosvenor Square, received his mother's letter with mixed feelings. Her visits to town were rare these days and, while he was happy to do his duty by her, the endless round of social engagements that she predicted was not something he looked forward to. He had suffered a severe disappointment in his youth, the lady in question having given him to understand that, had he not been possessed of a title and a considerable fortune, she would not have glanced twice in his direction. "How fortunate that, in addition to your handsome countenance and kind nature, you are blessed with considerable wealth," she had said coquettishly, tapping his arm with her folded fan. At first he had thought she was teasing, but he was soon to realise where her true ambition lay. Thankful that he had not reached the point of offering his hand, he had since been careful not to let down his guard. The experience had, for a while, given him a distaste for female companionship. While he speedily overcame this, the members of the fairer sex whom he favoured with his attention were of a different order to his own. The cynicism with which his calf love had left him had long since dissipated, but he'd had no cause to change the decision to retain his single state in the ensuing years. He was well aware that he was obliged, as head of his house, to marry and produce an heir, but it had always seemed to him that there was plenty of time to consider that. Meanwhile, he was a genial if somewhat distant companion.

In her letter, his mother had written:

I know I can rely on you, Rufus, for you are an accomplished dancer and a charming host. Lydia is lucky to have the support of such a brother. Did I mention that Miss Clifford comes with us to London? She has wonderful organisational abilities and will be of great assistance to me, I am certain. There's a sad tale there somewhere, of that I have no doubt. The family situation is not a happy one, but she is a delightful girl and I am happy to be able to assist her. Would you believe that awful woman did not even bring her to town to make her debut? She has spent her whole life within the confines of Buckinghamshire! Now, where was I? Ah, yes. We will arrive on the twenty-seventh of November or thereabouts. Do not feel obliged to welcome us, for I have made the housekeeper aware. I tell you only so that you should be forewarned of our coming.

Rufus laid aside the letter with a sigh. His peaceful existence was about to be curtailed, for the time being at least. His attendance at those social events from which he usually tried so hard to abstain could not be avoided, though he always behaved impeccably when obliged to attend. Nonetheless, mothers on the lookout for a handsome husband for their daughters had learned that it was dangerous to read anything into his behaviour. He treated all alike, with charm and friendliness, but no hopeful mother any longer aspired to welcoming him as her son-in-law, and he was looked upon with caution. What gentlemen did away from the eyes of their womenfolk was not something that was discussed in polite circles, but Rufus Solgrave was known to have had more than one light of love under his protection in the past. They were not, however, the sort of girls one might meet in his mother's drawing room. He wrote back to Elizabeth.

My dearest Mama,

You find me settled in London for the time being. I am sure Lydia must be eagerly looking forward to her come-out, and naturally I shall be happy to do whatever I can to ease her way into Society.

I was surprised to learn that Miss Clifford is to come with you. I hope she is by now fully recovered and I look forward to meeting her. She sent me a very pretty letter of thanks when I returned her locket (did she tell you?) and I am sure you are right in thinking that her presence will be of help both to you and to Lydia.

Do please tell my little sister that I cannot believe she is of an age to be presented. I still remember when we climbed trees together.

With affection,

Luxton

Though Rufus was indeed settled in London as he had told his mama, it transpired that on the day of the ladies' arrival at Solgrave House he was away from home, having journeyed some distance with Oliver Bridlington to a cockfight. They had discovered a rather charming inn where they'd decided to spend the night, both feeling rather too bosky to attempt the drive home. It was perhaps just as well that the earl was not present when his home was descended upon by three women in various stages of excitement, together with their entourage which took some time to disperse. By the time he arrived home the following afternoon, they were settled in and all was calm once more.

Having tried on one of her new gowns, Lydia was twirling in front of her mama in the morning room, and turned to look over her shoulder to see what reaction it had produced. It was at that very moment that Rufus entered the room. She was the first to see him.

"My dear," he said, pausing on the threshold. "Can this truly be my little sister? You will have the world at your feet, Lydia, for you look delightful."

"Rufus! How lovely to see you. Do you think so indeed?" she said, rushing to embrace him.

"Not," said her mother, "if you behave like a schoolgirl and with such a lack of modesty." But she was smiling. "Welcome home, son." She had risen and turned at Lydia's words, as had Sophie. "You must allow me to introduce you to Miss Clifford who, as you are aware, has been kind enough to join us for the Season."

Sophie looked at the earl with interest. A calm and self-possessed young lady, she showed none of the excitement her young friend had displayed and waited for him to move forward to greet her. Rufus was rooted to the spot, an arrested look on his face as his first thought was, *Her eyes are green.* He realised that he had wanted to know ever since he had seen them closed to the world. Awake, Sophie was even more beautiful than he remembered. She was taller than her companions and reached a little above his shoulders. Her trim figure was enhanced by a dress which fitted neatly under the bust before falling away in soft folds of pale green crepe. He quickly regained his composure, but not before the colour had risen in her cheeks at his obvious attention. Mentally berating himself for putting her to the blush, he said, "It is a pleasure to meet you and to know that you are now well, Miss Clifford."

"And I am happy at last to have the opportunity to thank you in person for saving me. Who knows how long I might have lain upon the ground if you had not come by?"

He placed an affectionate salute on his mother's cheek before disclaiming any heroism. "Your horse was standing guard over you. I am certain she would have waylaid any traveller on the road. I count myself fortunate it was me."

"Rufus, perhaps you might ring the bell for some tea and we can all sit down, unless you have something more pressing to do."

He assured Elizabeth that he was at the ladies' disposal and enquired as to what were their immediate plans. She replied that, prior to his arrival and Lydia's pirouette, she had been in the process of writing to her particular friends to inform them that she was once more in town. "And shortly I have the intention of holding a soirée and one or two small parties, prior to holding a ball in your sister's honour. You have no objection?"

"Of course not. This is your home as much as Ashby and you must do as you please."

He turned once more to Sophie. "Your mare has beautiful manners, Miss Clifford. Have you had her long?"

"For three years now and she is as gentle as they come, though as brave as a lion. I am fortunate that your mother has permitted me to bring her with me to London. She said there could be no objection."

"And she was right. I shall look forward to riding with you in the park, if you will permit?"

"The pleasure will be mine, and Snowflake's, of course."

He turned to his sister. "You may not be aware that I keep a box at the theatre. Would you care to go? I can arrange for a small party if you like, though I'm not sure what is on at present."

Lydia clapped her hands. "I care not what it is! It is kind of you to think of it, for it has been a long-held ambition of mine."

"Then I shall arrange it. You will join us, Mama? Miss Clifford?"

Secretly the countess was delighted that Rufus was making such an effort on Lydia's behalf, though she suspected the presence of the beautiful Sophie might also have had some bearing on what was evidently an impulsive offer. "What a delightful scheme. I'm sure both Lydia and Miss Clifford will enjoy the experience immensely, neither ever having been before."

Rufus was astonished and shot a look of enquiry at Sophie before remembering she had not been out of Buckinghamshire before. But she said with composure, "It is my first visit to London also, sir, and I shall be as delighted as your sister to join your party."

"Then I shall see to it immediately. Now, ladies, if you will excuse me…" He went to change his clothes, for he had arranged to meet Freddie Conroy in Bond Street.

They saw little of Luxton over the next two days. He dined at his club or was out with friends. He had, however, not forgotten his promise and popped into the drawing room one morning to ask the ladies if they would be free to join him that evening when there was to be a performance of Shakespeare's *Macbeth*, followed by a farce. Elizabeth assured her son that they would be ready at the designated time and, as soon as her brother had left, Lydia dragged her friend upstairs to decide what they would wear. Both young women were excited as never before, though it manifested itself in different ways. Lydia had no other subject of conversation for the remainder of the day, several times exclaiming, "I cannot wait." Sophie, on the other hand, was less overt about her feelings, though she was aware of a bubble of anticipation such as was entirely new to her.

To the surprise of the ladies, the carriage arrived at the exact time Rufus had designated. To his surprise, they were ready. Upon entering the carriage, Elizabeth asserted that the girls might anticipate having a wonderful time. Neither doubted they would.

Rufus, for not entirely unselfish reasons, had invited Bridlington and Conroy to join them and it was a merry party of people who settled themselves in Luxton's box for the younger ladies' first proper London outing. Sophie was introduced to the two friends, Lydia having met them previously on their not infrequent visits to Ashby. This was helpful in calming her nerves for, excitable as she was, she knew that a certain behaviour would be expected of her and she was at ease in their company. Sophie had no such qualms. Her social experience had been confined to a few families in Buckinghamshire, but she had been out for a few years now and did not suffer the pangs of trepidation that her friend was undergoing, though to Lydia's credit she hid it well.

"Miss Clifford, may I say what a pleasure it is to meet you," Oliver said as he bowed over her hand. "You must know that I am aware of your recent accident, for Luxton here told us all about it when finally he joined us in Leicestershire. I trust you are now fully recovered?"

Sophie laughed, replying, "From all but the ignominy of being unseated. It will take my pride some time, I fear, to recover from that."

"My understanding was that you may have come off worse after an encounter with an overhanging branch."

"Well, at least that will save my blushes."

Bridlington turned to remind Lydia of his success on his last visit to Ashby in providing dinner for the assembled company, "for your brother's trout stream is second to none," and Freddie stepped forward to take his place next to Sophie. He was, in his choice of apparel, far more restrained than his friend, the colours he wore muted but elegant, matching his quieter manner. She liked him immediately.

"I understand your mare made a great impression on Luxton. I would give much to meet her, for he is a great judge of horseflesh."

"And so you may, Mr Conroy. I am lucky enough to have been permitted to bring her with me to London and I hope to ride her in the park."

"Excellent! Would tomorrow be too soon?"

Something resembling a gurgle emanated from her throat as she replied, "Now you will think it was my intention to engage your company. I assure you, sir, though your manners are impeccable, that there is no need for such an instant invitation."

"Which in all honour I can now hardly retract. Do not disappointment me, Miss Clifford, when you have just complimented me on my address."

"Disappointment it must be, I am afraid, for I know that every moment of the day has already been accounted for." At this, he looked crestfallen. "But I believe the day after is free." He smiled once more.

A hush fell on the theatre as the play was about to begin, but Luxton had overheard the exchange and thought her charming, as indeed did his friends. In fact, Rufus spent little time watching the stage, his attention being on both his sister and her companion. He was as fond of Lydia as it was possible to be, the difference in their ages having throughout her childhood kept them from the squabbles that sometimes afflict siblings. She stared in rapt concentration, totally captivated by what was happening before her. Sophie's eyes too never left the players, and she leaned slightly forward in an unconscious effort to be as close to the stage as possible. She had, he thought, an air of assurance and a calmness about her that made him wonder at the friendship between her and his sister, so different were their personalities.

When the first act came to an end, Lydia and his two friends moved to speak to the countess, which gave Rufus his first opportunity to engage with his guest.

"You are enjoying the play, I trust."

She smiled. "I'm not sure that 'enjoying' is the right description. I found myself on tenterhooks throughout and am relieved to have a short respite."

"Perhaps the farce that follows will be more to your liking."

"I am sure I shall like them equally, for both are a novelty and it is my intention to savour every moment."

"And will you have to try hard, do you think?" he said, his smile reflecting her own.

"Oh no. There is so much going on. It was kind of you to arrange this evening for Lydia. She is having a wonderful time, don't you think?"

"I do think it, but it was arranged as much for you and my mother, who I know loves the theatre and rarely has the opportunity to indulge this pleasure. But come. What a dreadful host I am. Having organised refreshments, I am now giving you no opportunity of sampling them."

"Thank you, I find good conversation the greater sustenance."

By God, she was charming. She was not dissembling, he was sure. There was nothing but honesty in those beautiful green eyes. For the first time in many years Rufus found himself looking to one of his own social standing rather than the ladies of easy virtue he was wont, and safe, to associate with. There was no doubt that Miss Clifford was enchanting. No question either that she might be hanging out for a rich husband. She was wealthy in her own right. That much he already knew about her. Being familiar with the play he found, during the second act, that his thoughts were entirely focused upon her. He tried very hard to conjure up a vision of the delectable Fanny, the young woman at present under his protection. It was to no avail. All he could see was a pair of expressive green eyes set in an alabaster face framed by the most stunning red hair he had ever beheld. It would not do. She was residing in his home, under his mother's care. Even had he wanted to pursue her, and the very idea startled him because of its uniqueness, he could not do so. He must maintain his distance while inevitably seeing much of her. He had not even the luxury of removing himself. Had he not promised to aid his mother as much as he could in establishing his sister in Society? And in any case, he would not leave Lydia at such a time. He was far too fond of her and would enjoy watching her transition as she became more accustomed to London ways. But with Lydia's changes would come those of Sophie Clifford. Rufus smiled ruefully as he realised that, for the first time since his youth, he was seriously drawn to another woman.

At the play's end, and before the farce, he took the opportunity to resume their conversation.

"I could not help but overhear you earlier arranging to ride with Conroy. I hope you will not object if I join you. We could go together to meet him."

"Of course I wouldn't object. I wondered how I might get there. I am unfamiliar with the protocol but fully aware that I should not go alone. I am sure Lydia too would wish to ride, but her horse threw a splint the day before we left and she had to leave him behind, though I believe he is to follow us in a few days."

"There is one horse here which is suitable for her, whom she has in fact ridden in the past. I keep her for when my mother visits, though she rarely rides these days. What do you think, Lydia?" he said, addressing his sister. "Would you care to ride in the park? Conroy has engaged to go with Miss Clifford the day after tomorrow, and I know how much you enjoy the activity."

"If Bunny is still in your stable, I should be delighted."

"It is agreed, then."

The evening had exceeded all their expectations, and there had been a lively discussion in the carriage on the way home as to which had been the most entertaining, the play or the farce.

Several invitations had by now been received by the countess, who told the girls, "We shall be gay to dissipation." Appointments were made with dressmakers and milliners to add to the finery they had brought with them to town. Most important of all was Lydia's gown for her coming out ball and much thought had been given to its design. Fair-haired but with a creamy complexion, she was able to wear white without it chasing all the colour from her face, though yellow made her look sallow. They had pored over several designs while still in Buckinghamshire and Lydia had a good idea of what she wanted. It remained to be seen what the dressmaker would say. Sophie had chosen ivory silk and her only ornament was to be her mother's locket. The morning found Elizabeth and her charges setting out to visit various establishments, none the worse for the gaiety of the previous late evening.

"I love London, Mama. Did I tell you that?"

"You may have mentioned it once or twice, Lydia. I have to acknowledge that there is about the place something that heightens one's senses. And you, Sophie — has the city embraced you as well?"

"I'm sure one could spend a lifetime here and not be bored. I always thought of myself as a countrywoman, but there is so much to see and do."

"The first of which involves getting ourselves suitably kitted out, and here is Madame Clara's shop. Come, girls. There is much to be done."

Armed with their drawings, they were delighted when their suggestions met with approval. There would be minor changes, of course, but on the whole the dressmaker considered both ladies had chosen well. Roses fashioned out of lemon satin would adorn the deep hem and short full sleeves of Lydia's gown. More would be woven into her hair, and the whole would be set off by a shawl of net silk of the same colour.

Madame Clara was delighted to have two such beautiful young women to attire. To Sophie, she said, "We must have a double row of small green bows just beneath the bodice, and the same on the sleeves. Ribbons in your hair will mirror the hue. Yes, and a silk shawl to match. You have beautiful eyes, if I may be permitted to say so, and we must make the most of them." She turned to Lady Luxton. "They will look charming, the young ladies, *n'est-ce pas*? And am I to fashion a gown for you, my lady?"

"Most certainly you are. You have dressed me before and I look to you to suggest something that will have other mothers staring with envy," she said. "Nothing outrageous, you understand, but *quelque chose* with a *je ne sais quoi*."

"You may rely on me, Lady Luxton."

Sophie and Lydia were called upon to comment on Madame's suggestions for Elizabeth but could find no fault. The woman's taste was impeccable. The countess, well-satisfied, ushered them out, pausing only to arrange a time for the first fitting. There were shoes, reticules, fans, gloves and all manner of things remaining to be purchased.

"These shops are far superior to any I have seen in Buckinghamshire," Sophie said.

"Yes, Madame Fleur, of the stupid name which is so obviously adopted, does well enough, but they are far more professional here," Elizabeth replied.

There was a moment, albeit fleeting, when Sophie felt resentment stir at having been denied these pleasures for so long and never having been given, in her opinion, an adequate reason. However, she was not one to lament over something she could not change. There was time enough to catch up.

"Sufficient for one day, I think," said Elizabeth. "When you are out riding tomorrow, I shall turn my attention to expanding on details for your ball, Lydia. Simpson and I have much to discuss. She is finding that there is a vast difference between looking to the needs of a single gentleman about town and the household duties necessary to entertain on the scale we are anticipating. I have to say, I was concerned prior to our arrival. Though she has always been accommodating in the past, she has never undertaken anything on this scale. I am pleasantly surprised at both her enthusiasm and efficiency."

"Is there anything I can do to help?" asked Sophie. "You promised I might. In fact, I remember making it a condition of my accompanying you, to assuage the pangs of guilt I might have had for taking advantage of your hospitality."

"Rest assured, my dear, if there were I would have no hesitation in asking. However, you are my guest and my only wish is that you should attain as much pleasure as you are able from your visit."

Sophie judged that it would not be a difficult task and said so. "And I cannot thank you sufficiently."

"Nonsense!"

CHAPTER FIVE

The two young women caused no small stir almost from the moment they entered Hyde Park the following day. Conroy joined them soon enough and was lavish in his praise of Snowflake.

"She is everything I was led to believe, Miss Clifford. How did you come by her?"

Her chin rose a fraction. In the past her knowledge had been brought into question by Follet who, if his own horses were anything to judge by, could be taken for a flat. It had made her defensive and she replied, "I chose her myself. I am country-bred and hope I know one end of a horse from the other. There is no way I would allow anyone else to choose my mount for me."

"Then I make you my compliments. She is a beauty."

Sophie smiled and dropped her chin, always pleased to accept praise on behalf of her favourite. "You must forgive me for being short with you, Mr Conroy. In my experience, men have always believed mere females to be incapable of judging horseflesh. I'm afraid I was a little rude."

"Not at all, and I am happy to reassure you that I am not of their number. You are a woman of surprises, Miss Clifford."

"Not I, sir. I am nothing out of the ordinary."

If he chose not to agree with her, he didn't say so.

Bridlington reined in beside them some half an hour after their arrival, having also been present at the theatre when the outing was mooted. Adept at doing the pretty without setting up false hopes in any young woman's breast, he was felt to be an asset to any group.

"Good morning, ladies. Luxton. Conroy. You look delightful, Miss Clifford," he said, "though the green of your habit fades into insignificance beside the colour of your eyes."

"Oh, Lord Bridlington, have you nothing as charming to say to me?" Lydia asked teasingly and with a flutter of her lashes, at ease with this friend of her brother because of their many previous meetings.

"I can only say, Miss Solgrave, that the sky which I had previously thought a bright blue is but pale by comparison to your own sapphire orbs."

She laughed delightfully. Young and inexperienced though Lydia was, Rufus had no fear that these compliments would turn her head and inwardly thanked his lucky stars that she had spent enough time with the opposite sex not to be thrown into a state of confusion by a few fulsome remarks. It would stand her in good stead in the coming weeks, he was sure.

"It is beyond me, Ollie, how you can manage to flirt with two women at the same time and not give offence to either," he said.

"Practice, dear boy. Practice."

Rufus and Oliver, with Sophie between them, took up the lead while Conroy and Lydia followed close behind. They were halted many times by acquaintances of one or other of the three gentleman, asking to be introduced to their companions. It was altogether delightful except for one thing. It marred Sophie's enjoyment and caused concern to her host, for it became evident that she was drawing no little interest from passers-by who turned their heads to look at her. She could only put it down to town manners but deemed it rude. She did not like to be stared at. Rufus, however, knew that this was not normal behaviour and wondered what it was about his guest that was arousing so much interest. It wasn't until much later, after Sophie and Lydia had returned to Grosvenor Square and the three friends had gone to their club, that he was enlightened by his friend Ollie.

"Must have been the hair, dear boy. Only ever seen one other with a mane that particular shade of red. Expect that's what everyone was thinking. You remember what Pontonby said when we were in Leicestershire. She don't have his features, but I'll lay you a monkey there's a connection to Joseph Templeton."

It was an unwelcome disclosure and wasn't something that had previously occurred to Luxton, not being acquainted with the man in question. Now, with it being pointed out to him so succinctly, he could not deny its probable truth.

"Miss Clifford is a guest of my mother, Bridlington," he replied, almost tersely. "I would thank you not to repeat such gossip while she remains under my roof. If there is any truth in your suggestion, I am certain as I can be that the lady in question is entirely unaware, and I would prefer that it remain that way."

"Certainly, old boy. Mum's the word. I wouldn't have said anything if you hadn't mentioned it yourself."

Rufus tried to put the matter to the back of his mind, but there was no doubting that if people had remarked on the resemblance on Sophie's first outing, it was something that would recur in the future. It left him feeling uneasy.

"Would you object greatly, my darling, if I were to invite the Vaughans to Lydia's ball? I know Mrs Vaughan in particular never fails to irritate you."

"Good gracious, Mama, you must invite whomsoever you please. With luck I may greet her in the hall and thereafter have no further need to speak to her."

He was smiling, for he well knew she would seek him out as she did whenever they met. He was always too polite to give a rebuff and could not understand her persistence. She was one of the few who had tried to promote her daughter to him, but that young lady was now married, happily he hoped, so there seemed no reason to pursue the connection.

"Well, I only ask because, unlike those occasions when you have met at other people's parties, you will not, at this one, have the opportunity to remove yourself and the woman is like a leech."

"You do me an injustice. I long ago learned how to deal with such encroaching busybodies. I was taught by an expert, after all. Papa was used to say you were too high in the instep. I never agreed with him, but you are most certainly mistress of the art of put-down."

Elizabeth accepted what he said as a compliment, as he had intended she should. She was still laughing when she began to speak about the number of candles to be ordered and asked if he would like to discuss the menu with her.

"Oh no, Mama, do not draw me in. I am happy to provide Solgrave House and whatever you consider suitable to give Lydia as spectacular an evening as she could hope for, but do not expect to embroil me in the finer details. I give you carte blanche and promise only to be here on the day to give whatever support you and my sister require."

"And Miss Clifford, of course, for while we cannot be said to be launching her into Society it will be an opportunity for her as well. I like the girl and I know she is not happy at home. I would hope we can find an eligible suitor, for she is a capable woman and would do far better in her own home."

Rufus found that he had mixed feelings. To himself he acknowledged that he was strongly attracted to Sophie. The thought of putting her in the way of another man did not appeal, but he merely answered his mother, "Yes, and Miss Clifford," before leaving her to her planning and going off to Bond Street in the hope of a round in the ring with Gentleman Jackson, a privilege not granted to just anyone, but the famous boxer had been kind enough to spar with him in the past.

Sophie was enjoying herself immensely. The almost daily visits to some emporium or other to purchase a shawl, some slippers, trimmings and other accessories were a source of great pleasure. It wasn't only a new gown or other larger items she delighted in. The acquisition of a set of buttons to trim the sleeves of a pelisse sent her back to Grosvenor Square determined to sew them on immediately, and she was not disappointed with the result.

"I don't know how you have the patience to do that, and they are so evenly placed," Lydia said when asked to look and see if she did not think it a great improvement. "I cannot tell you the number of times that I have been told by my governess to unpick my stitches and begin again. And look how neat your workbasket is! My threads are always muddled such that I can never find what I'm looking for. Not that I look very often," she added laughingly, "for it is a task I avoid as much as possible."

"You must consider our different circumstances, Lydia. When at Charnwood I was obliged to sit with Mama for some hours each day, to bear her company, you understand. To this day I do not know why, for neither of us found pleasure in being with the other. However, at least when I had my sewing box I could be usefully employed and the concentration that was required removed me one step from her inane chatter. You, on the other hand, have always had a delightful companion in the countess. But forgive me, I must sound inexcusably disloyal."

Lydia could only be sad for her friend but Sophie had been content enough, never having known anything else, and her daily rides with Snowflake had aided in retaining her sanity. It would not be so in the future, she knew. Having tasted life, she dreaded returning to Buckinghamshire to be once more incarcerated. Though she sat quietly sewing, thoughts were running through her mind as to how she could avoid such a circumstance. She was wealthy enough to be independent of her childhood home but, at twenty-one years of age, she would be thought eccentric in the extreme if she were to set up on her own, even with a female companion. She could not, nonetheless, dismiss the idea once it had occurred. But did she have the courage? She determined to put it to the back of her mind, for she had weeks still in London and would not allow thoughts of her future to spoil her present enjoyment.

Sophie and Lydia had already attended a number of social engagements in Elizabeth's company — small affairs, for her mother would not allow Lydia to appear at any large function or anyone else's ball before her own. Two invitations had been declined with no little regret, but the countess would not be swayed.

"You cannot attend a ball without wearing a ball gown, my darling, and to purchase two would be an extravagance even I could not justify. You can surely see in any case that your first appearance must be at the head of the stairs here in Grosvenor Square, or in the hall as we greet our guests."

There was no denying the logic of this statement and the girls acquiesced without further argument. In truth, their presence at smaller gatherings was a much cannier way of introducing them into Society. Sophie was older and more self-assured. Lydia was delightfully young and excitable but, due to her association with her brother's friends and her mother's careful upbringing, well-behaved and seemingly demure. Both were above average height and their features and colouring, though different, were sufficient to attract people to their sides to learn more of the newcomers. Rufus had been engaged to join them at a soirée given by a particular friend of his mother with whom he had been acquainted since childhood. Finding it impossible to refuse, he had then to watch others paying court to the woman with whom he was fast becoming obsessed. Standing beside him was Lady Jersey, one of the patronesses of Almack's, in whom lay the authority to bestow or withhold vouchers for that establishment, the key to any young woman's success.

"They look delightful, do they not, Luxton?" she remarked. "Your sister will be a hit for sure, and Miss Clifford is an outstanding beauty. It is to be hoped the colour of her hair will not hold her back."

"You do not like red hair, Sally?" he demanded, one eyebrow raised in question. Though others might walk in fear of the great power wielded by these arbiters, Rufus stood on terms of friendship with Lady Jersey and did not seek to be conciliatory when speaking with her.

"Do not be ingenuous, Rufus. Or can it be that you are unaware…"

He interrupted her, not wishing to open up this line of conversation. "It is always refreshing to talk to you, my dear. I had worried that this party might be insipid, but I must say I am enjoying myself thoroughly. Will you permit me to introduce you to my sister and her friend?"

It was dangerous. Lady Jersey could, if she chose, be as haughty as she wished. There was a slight hesitation, but she chose instead to be amused. She took his arm. "I should be delighted."

Aware that he had been holding his breath and, worse, that he had risked his mother's ambitions, Luxton led her to where all three were seated. They rose as they were approached, but Sally insisted they be seated again and demanded of Rufus, "A chair, if you will, so that I may sit and talk with your mother and her companions."

She chatted with them for some minutes, asking them if they were enjoying London and all the treats they had thus far experienced.

"We seem to go from one delight to another, Lady Jersey," Sophie said. "I certainly did not appreciate how busy we would be or how much pleasure I would take from the experience."

"And you, Miss Solgrave, your coming out ball is to take place next week, I understand?"

"It is, and I cannot thank Mama sufficiently for all she has done."

"Very prettily said, my dear. No doubt you will want vouchers for Almack's as well. I shall see that you receive them. Now, if you'll excuse me, I see someone approaching whom I most wish to avoid." She arose and left them, a sideways look at Luxton which was full of mischief and seeming to ask if he was not now satisfied.

His mother was delighted and told the girls quietly, "You have one foot in the door now. I could not have wished for more."

Following Lady Jersey's approbation, it seemed the number of morning visitors who called at Grosvenor Square increased tenfold, for where she went few failed to follow. One would never know it to observe her, but Elizabeth was at once in a state of deep contentment and high anxiety. Everything was exceeding her expectations and it was a gracious lady who received each in turn. Posies too were left at the door when the three were not at home. And Luxton exclaimed one day, "If I fall over another young man in the hall, I shall renege on all my promises and flee to Ashby."

"Your club is far closer, should you become desperate," his mother said with fondness. She knew Rufus would never desert her in her time of need.

Arrangements for the ball were going as planned, for the countess had been preparing for months. It did not stop her checking each day with her housekeeper to ensure that the required number of candles had been delivered, that every glass droplet in the chandeliers in the ballroom was sparkling, that the silver was gleaming. The flower order was checked. The menu also, again and again. Conversations took place with the cook, and people from outside had been engaged to aid him. Bedchambers were prepared and inspected in readiness for those who were to remain overnight; a cousin and his wife from Harrogate and a family from Bath. All went on behind the scenes. In the morning room, everything was calm. They never knew whom next to expect, but perhaps the last person they thought to see arrived only the day before the ball.

"Mr Follet, my lady," said the footman, showing Francis into the room. It was fortunate that others were present or Sophie might have discredited herself, so cross was she that he had come. He was charm personified, but in an ingratiating way that caused her to feel positively ill and such was her dislike of him that she was ashamed when he was introduced to the rest as her brother. She could not help but compare his manners with those of Lord Luxton, so much more refined and well-bred. Follet, it seemed, was determined to outstay all the other guests and the reason became clear when he was at last alone with the family.

"You will forgive me, I am sure, Lady Luxton. I could not remain in Buckinghamshire while my sister and her friend are to celebrate in such a fashion. I am family, after all," he said with a smirk that made all but himself feel exceedingly uncomfortable. "I was hoping, with such a large house, that you might accommodate me during my stay. I have seen to it that my luggage was deposited in your hall."

It was fortunate, since Lydia, Sophie and even Elizabeth were rendered speechless, that Rufus had entered the room in time to hear this.

"I'm sorry to disappoint you, Follet," he said jovially, "but all the accommodation has already been allocated to other visitors who will be travelling considerable distances. Had we known you were coming, of course ... but I don't recall your name being on the list? Let me recommend Grillon's in Albemarle Street, or perhaps the Clarendon." As set-downs go, it was exquisite. In such a vast house there would always be a chamber to spare, but no-one could have accused the earl of rudeness.

Follet was left only able to mumble, "I must apologise. I did not think. Naturally, if you do not have room."

He rose to leave, and Rufus offered with barely a change of expression but with a definite twitch in the corner of his mouth, "You may of course leave your luggage here until you have resolved where you are to stay." He then, in the ladies' opinions, spoiled it all by saying, "Naturally, we would be delighted to see you at the ball tomorrow."

He saw the intruder out and returned to the morning room to be greeted by Sophie with, "How could you, Lord Luxton? You are aware how much I dislike my brother."

"The man is vulgar to say the very least, but I had little option, Miss Clifford. Only think what might be said when it is known he is in town and did not put in an appearance tomorrow. There would have been no call for comment had he remained at Charnwood, but he did not. I would not have anything reflect badly upon you, or indeed my mother. I will do my best to ensure he does not embarrass you."

Sophie smiled, for she could see his argument. "False hope, I fear, but I thank you."

CHAPTER SIX

Sophie was, in her much quieter and more dignified way, equally as excited as Lydia. When Bertha drew back the curtains on the morning of the ball, the sun came streaming in through the window. She sat up in bed and accepted a cup of hot chocolate with enthusiasm.

"You must be that excited, Miss Sophie. Your first ball."

Sophie laughed but protested, "I have been to one or two in Buckinghamshire, you must recall, though not of course on this scale. In any case, it's not my ball, Bertha, but Miss Lydia's."

Bertha knew otherwise. While the focus was naturally upon the younger girl, today would be as big a day in her mistress's life as she had ever seen. "That's as may be, miss, but I suggest you stir yourself, for we have much to do."

There was not a spare moment between then and the arrival of the first guests, those who had come from out of town. The final touches had been put to the ballroom early in the day and the countess made her inspection before taking breakfast. A hush fell over the vast room, situated at the back of the house and overlooking the garden, as her staff held their breath, waiting, praying for approval. After a long pause it came, the delay being on account of the overwhelming emotion Elizabeth was feeling. She turned her back to the splendour and faced the small group of people.

"You have done me proud, and I thank every one of you. Now, off with you all, for there is still much to be done."

They dispersed and she turned once more to face the large windows, draped in gold damask which was duplicated in the coverings of the dainty chairs that lined the walls. The walls to her right and left were hung with large mirrors which reflected huge crystal chandeliers, sparkling even before the candles had been lit. In the centre a large square had been marked out for dancing and music stands had been set up in the far left-hand corner ready for the arrival of the musicians. Elizabeth was pulled from her reverie by the arrival of her son, who stood beside her and put his arm around her shoulders.

"Satisfied, Mama?"

"It will be spectacular, my boy. You will lead your sister out for the first dance?"

"Naturally. And I hope you will approve, for I have purchased new evening dress especially for the occasion," he said teasingly.

She turned to look at him, her features serious for a moment. "Do you mind, Rufus? We have descended upon you and taken over your home. You are a man of action and, while I am proud to say that your company at any social occasion is an asset, it is not what comes most naturally to you, is it?"

"Mama, I adore you. Of course I don't mind, and just because I don't do the pretty very often does not mean I am incapable of enjoying it when I do. Rest assured, I am looking forward to this evening with as much anticipation as you and Lydia and Miss Clifford, if only so I may crush the pretentions of that dreadful man, Follet. Now come and join me for breakfast."

Sophie saw little of Elizabeth and Lydia for the first part of the day. The countess was busy not only with the finishing touches but also with her house guests. Her daughter, when invited by Sophie to go riding, said she would stay close to her mother in case of need, but for Miss Clifford there was little to do regarding the arrangements and she was loth to forego her daily ride. Intending to venture out with only her groom for company, she was delighted when Luxton offered to accompany her.

"My mother has kindly but firmly dismissed me. 'I shall require your presence only this evening, Rufus,' she said to me. 'You may go and amuse yourself elsewhere if you please.' As you may imagine, I felt as if I were a boy again and sent to play with my toys."

"I too would like to have been of assistance, but Lady Luxton wouldn't hear of it. And Snowflake would certainly wonder if I were not to arrive as usual," she said, a smile playing around her mouth as it did whenever she spoke of her favourite.

"Then we need have no conscience. I can be ready in half an hour if that meets with your approval."

Though the day was cool at this time of year, the sun continued to shine out of a clear blue sky, just as it had when Bertha had drawn the curtains earlier in the day. The horses walked side by side, and the easy companionship that had been established during her stay in London allowed Sophie to converse with Rufus as if their friendship had been long-established. Her smile was somewhat rueful when she said, "I must thank you again, sir, for your handling of an awkward situation, though I confess I was a little displeased yesterday when you invited my brother to the ball."

"A little displeased! I fear that, had you a dagger to hand, I would have been a dead man."

"No, how can you say that? I am no believer in violence. I would have found some other means to avenge myself."

They broke into a trot, laughing, before continuing in silence, enjoying the pleasure of being out on such a fine day. Walking once more, they were hailed by several people who exchanged greetings with them, one or two of whom expressed their delighted anticipation of the coming evening. Freddie Conroy was one and turned his horse to ride alongside of them.

"You should have seen Oliver last evening, Rufus. He had promised to join me this morning, but I'm not surprised to find him absent. I suspect he is nursing quite a headache. He was dipping rather deep, you know. I only hope he may be sober enough to come to your party this evening, Miss Clifford."

"I have not been acquainted with Lord Bridlington for long but, from the little I know of him, it would take much for him to forego a party. In any case, I have promised to dance with him. He is far too much the gentleman to disappoint me." All at once the smile fled and her expression changed to one of dismay. "Oh no! There is my brother. On the strut and no doubt looking to see whom he might impress."

"In that case," said Rufus, smiling to himself at her use of so unladylike an expression, "it is time to allow the horses to stretch their legs once more. We must, all three of us, avert our eyes as we pass and pretend we haven't seen him."

The day flew by so fast that the time to get dressed seemed to come around almost before they were ready. Bertha had brushed Sophie's hair until it gleamed. With her curls dressed, two or three falling on her left shoulder, and the satin ribbon woven through them, it was time to put on her gown. The green bows beneath the bodice were reflected in a band at the hem. They created a perfect balance and, set against the ivory silk, she could not wish for more. Bertha sniffed. Sophie smiled.

"Now, don't upset yourself. You have seen me dressed in my finery before now."

"Yes, miss, but never like his. You look like a princess; that you do."

Sophie was well satisfied and went along the corridor to her friend's room to see how she was progressing. Elizabeth was with her, and Lydia was in her underdress and just about to step into her gown.

"Come in, come in," the countess said, almost abruptly in her anxiety, but she stopped when Sophie stepped forward. "My dear, you look charming. You will break hearts for sure. Now be careful, Lydia," she continued, turning her attention back to her daughter. "Do not step on the hem, for we can do without any last-minute repairs."

There was a hush for a moment as Miss Solgrave stood upright to face Elizabeth and Sophie. A vision in white, her dress arrayed with tiny rosebuds, she looked exactly as any debutante's mother might dream for her daughter, and Lady Luxton was no exception. There was a tear in her eye. "Charming. Absolutely charming," she whispered, emotion causing her voice to tremble. "It is time we joined our guests for dinner."

She was herself dressed in dusky pink brocade and, though the colour was suitable for both her age and status, her figure was still trim and she trod lightly. Rufus was waiting for them at the head of the stairs, resplendent in evening dress and ready to do his duty by the ladies. If they heard his sharp intake of breath, they could not know that it was as much on behalf of Sophie as Lydia. Elizabeth and Sophie preceded brother and sister and, after a suitable gap, it was left for Lord Luxton to escort Miss Solgrave down the sweeping staircase. Their visitors were waiting below, and the effect was everything a fond mama could have wished. Aside from those who were staying in Grosvenor Square, a few additional guests had been invited to the pre-ball dinner. Lady Jersey, perhaps because of her fondness for Lord Luxton, had graciously accepted the invitation and it was he who led her in to dine. Conroy and Bridlington, too, had been bidden, "for I shall need you both to help entertain the dullest set of relations a man ever had," Rufus had begged.

Some twenty persons gathered in the large dining room and were presented with a meal of which no Society hostess would have been ashamed. Freddie and Oliver were outstanding in keeping amused two cousins, both ladies of a condescending nature; a callow youth, the son of one of them; and an elderly gentleman who had little conversation but addressed himself to enjoying everything that was placed before him. Dinner over, they assembled in the large marble entrance hall where the countess, Lord Luxton and Miss Solgrave were to greet their guests. Sophie stood with Conroy and Bridlington as carriage after carriage drew up outside, and eventually they adjourned to the ballroom where, the candles having now been lit, a spectacular display awaited them all.

In no time it seemed the ballroom was so full it was difficult to pass from one side to another or to hear oneself speak.

Rufus led his sister onto the dancefloor and Sophie joined them a moment later in company with Oliver Bridlington. He had not let her down, though he admitted with a grin that it had been a close-run thing and that his head still ached from his excesses of the previous evening.

Others assembled and those who were not dancing either sat or circulated around the edge of the room. The ton had been summoned to Grosvenor Square and they had come, a compliment both to the countess and Lord Luxton. The first set at an end, Rufus did not join the second but performed his duties as host, ensuring that he spoke to every one of his guests and such was his charm that each felt he or she had been singled out. He was near the door when a latecomer arrived and, with no less civility but perhaps less sincerity, Rufus greeted Follet and bore him over to his mother, his sister and Miss Clifford. The man was unctuous in the extreme and when he begged Sophie for the next dance she looked, Luxton told her later, like a cornered rabbit.

"I fear I am before you, Follet. Your sister is promised to me and, if I mistake not, the musicians are just striking up. You will excuse us, of course."

He put out his hand and Sophie took it gratefully. Her brother had no choice but to stand back. As the couple took their places, Rufus looked at his partner with pure mischief writ upon his face. She was furious.

"Are you always to put me in an impossible situation, only to rescue me from it? You, sir, are abominable."

"And you, madam, are a delight."

The words were out before he could stop them and each was as shocked as the other. She was first to recover.

"Do not think you can play off your wiles against me. I have watched you this evening and it is my belief you could charm the most challenging of people. And I hope I am not that!"

Rufus, who was as close as he had ever been to a declaration he had no intention of making, found his sense of humour returning and replied, "Only sometimes."

"You are, you are…!" she spluttered.

"I know. You already said. Abominable." But the difficult moment had passed.

Sophie returned to Elizabeth's side, Lydia being engaged in conversation nearby with Conroy. "What a squeeze," she heard someone say nearby. Elizabeth also had heard the remark and knew the evening to be a success, for no greater accolade could there be.

Some of the gentlemen, feeling they had done their duty, disappeared to the card room, though there seemed little thinning of the company. Although it was winter, the moon was shining out of a clear sky and there were those who were minded to step out onto the terrace for a few moments to escape the heat in the ballroom. Follet was amongst them and, when Sophie wrapped a shawl about her shoulders and did the same, he confronted her. Aware that he would not leave her alone until he'd had his say, she moved with him to a bench away from the rest and sat down.

"Well, Francis, what is it you wish to say to me?"

"You must know how I feel about you, Sophie. An alliance between us would cement the relationship we have already through the marriage of my mother and —" he paused — "and your father. We have not always rubbed along well together, but such is often the case between siblings. However, I desire to be married and to set up my own nursery. I know you do not return my affection, but surely you can see how advantageous such a union would be to us both."

At the mention of children Sophie shuddered inwardly, and she could not help but marvel at his persistence when she had so often refused him. She tried a different approach. "I thank you for the honour you do me, Francis, and it does you credit that you desire a tightening of the ties between our respective parents. However, I cannot return your affection and I would beg you not to raise the subject again." *There*, she thought, *I have been as gentle as I was able, and perhaps he will now accept my refusal.* She was astonished therefore when he jumped to his feet and paced up and down before returning to face her.

"You will not get a better offer. Mark my words, you will regret this decision, for you have little chance under the circumstances of finding another to wed you."

"What circumstances, Francis? You persist in alluding to something of which it seems I have no knowledge. It is something, I recall, which you have done previously. Be plain with me now. What is it you are not telling me?"

"I have said too much. It is not for me to divulge… I will leave you now, and you have my word I will not renew my entreaties. If you should change your mind at any time, I will be more than happy to oblige you."

With that, he turned on his heel and walked away, leaving her alone on the terrace. *Oblige me! Condescending to say the least.* But there was no getting away from it. Sophie was shaken up, not by Francis's proposal, but by the inference that she was not in a position to make a suitable match. Stuck in the country, she had never given much thought to her eligibility as a bride and, while marriage had never been uppermost in her mind, she had, subconsciously perhaps, always assumed that the day would come when she would leave Charnwood as a married woman. But her brother was insinuating that would never be the case. What secret was there hidden in her past of which she was unaware and which might have such a devastating effect on her future? Suddenly cold, she rose from the bench and returned to the ballroom but she excused herself to Elizabeth, merely remarking that she would return shortly, and she went to her bedchamber. She needed time for some quiet reflection.

Luxton had observed her departure and, before it, that of Follet, who had not even stayed to thank his hosts. That

Sophie was disturbed might not be evident to the other guests, for her exit was unhurried and did not command attention. But Rufus could tell that something was amiss. Naturally he could not follow her, but he sincerely hoped she would soon recover from whatever had lowered her spirits and that he might have an opportunity to talk with her later. Soon it would be time to go into supper, and her absence would be remarked upon. Should it be necessary, he would ask Lydia to bring her back downstairs.

It was not necessary. Sophie looked in her glass and observed that, other than an abnormal pallor, she appeared as usual. After splashing her cheeks with a little water from the jug on the dresser, she took one very deep breath and returned to the ballroom just as Rufus was about to approach his sister. Thankful to see her back, he realised there would be no opportunity for a while to have any significant conversation with her. Supper was announced and he led his mother into the dining room. Fortunately, Sophie was escorted by Bridlington and, when a group formed, of which Lydia and Conroy were a part, he was content that she would be suitably entertained for such time as it might take for her to recover her composure.

CHAPTER SEVEN

The guests had gone. Those who were remaining until the next day had retired to their bedchambers, and four very tired but contented people sat down for one last nightcap before doing the same.

"Mama, Rufus, I cannot thank you sufficiently. It was even more wonderful than I had anticipated and people were so kind. It is an evening I shall remember my whole life."

Lydia's eyes were glowing with happiness and the added anticipation of visits from one or two young gentlemen who had begged the honour of calling upon her. Elizabeth was hardly less pleased. All her weeks of careful preparation had culminated in a ball which would be the talk of the ton for days to come. There had been nothing to mar the pleasure but the accidental breaking of one of her favourite Sevres vases by an overly-exuberant viscount who had flung wide his arms while describing the size of a fish he had recently caught. She looked ruefully at her son and made her apologies.

"It is a small price to pay, Mama, to see you and my sister so happy. I make you my compliments. I have little doubt that the knocker will be much used in the next few weeks. And you, Miss Clifford? Did you also find the evening met your expectations?"

It wasn't what he wanted to ask her. There had been no opportunity to enquire further as to her exchanges with her brother and the moment now had passed. He could not easily raise the subject and hoped she might confide in Lydia or Elizabeth about whatever it was that had distressed her.

Observing her now, one would never have imagined that she had earlier been so put out that she'd had to flee the ballroom.

"I can only add my thanks to those of all your other guests, though mine is the greatest debt. Never have I attended such a gathering and my hand was solicited for every single dance. What more could a woman ask?"

"I count myself lucky to have had the opportunity of dancing with you."

"And I that you rescued me from my odious brother. I make no apology for saying what must be obvious to all; that his company is not what one would choose. I had not realised until you were so kind as to invite me for a prolonged stay, Elizabeth, what an objectionable man he is. In fact, I am dreading having to return to Charnwood."

It was said with a smile, but not one of her listeners doubted the truth of her assertion.

"It may be that you are not required to do so, my dear," replied her hostess. "I feel certain that before the Season is over you will be promised to some fine gentleman who will devote himself to your welfare."

"It is kind of you to say so." It seemed to Rufus that Sophie was about to make some further comment, but she lowered her eyes and said no more. He would have given much to know what she was thinking.

True to Lord Luxton's prediction, a stream of visitors came to call upon the ladies in the ensuing days. Many invitations also arrived, and hardly an evening was spent at home. Conroy in particular was a frequent visitor in Grosvenor Square and could be found in the morning room far more often than his friendship with Rufus would give justification to. There was little doubt that he was quietly but determinedly paying court to Miss Solgrave. The countess smiled benignly upon him. She had known him for several years and had welcomed him often when he came into Buckinghamshire. A kind man with gentle manners, she thought he would do very well for her daughter, though for Lydia to be forming an attachment so early in her first Season was perhaps not quite desirable. Better for her to acquire some town bronze before committing to an engagement. As to that, Elizabeth was unable to tell whether her daughter felt any preference for this suitor above the others. She could only be glad that her manners were such that she conducted herself in a way her mother could be proud of.

One day when Sophie was walking in Hyde Park with Bridlington, Lydia and Conroy close behind, her attention was inexplicably drawn to a rider coming towards them. She had at the time been pointing out a tree which had evidently been laden with fruit, for much of it lay upon the ground beneath, when she saw a gentleman on a huge bay gelding, so tall that she had to look up to see his face. This she did at the exact same moment he glanced down at her, his expression arrested. He smiled and nodded before passing by. It unsettled her and she stopped in her tracks. Lydia, whose attention was firmly fixed on Freddie Conroy, very nearly bumped into her. Sophie laid a hand on Oliver's arm and looked questioningly at him.

"That man. The one who has just ridden by. I think I have not seen him before, but he seemed to acknowledge me as if we were acquainted. Pray, can you tell me who he is?"

Bridlington, whose gaze had been fixed on the tree, had not seen the rider. He looked over his shoulder to see who she was referring to. "Good Lord, is he back in town? I haven't seen him for years. We should move on, Miss Clifford, for I do believe we are causing an obstruction," he said, gripping her elbow and moving forward. She went willingly enough but repeated the question. "Why, that's Joseph Templeton," he answered. "He's been fixed abroad for an age. Frankly, I thought never to see him again."

"He looked surprised when he saw me. I couldn't help noticing. His hair, Lord Bridlington. Streaked with grey but nevertheless red. Very red. Like mine. I wondered if perhaps we might be connected in some way."

Ollie was no coward but he didn't think it fell to him to offer a full explanation, and certainly not in the middle of Hyde Park. "We all have the odd skeleton in the family cupboard. Got one myself. A right rum'n. I expect yours will turn out to be one too. But you seem out of sorts. Let me take you back to Grosvenor Square so that you may recover your composure."

He turned and explained to their companions that they were returning home because Miss Clifford was feeling a little faint. With Lydia's abigail in close attendance, there was no need for them to discontinue their walk.

"Oliver," Sophie said as they walked, using his given name for the first time, "the encounter has given me such an odd feeling. No doubt you are right. Perhaps he will turn out to be the black sheep of the family. I wonder who he is."

Sophie had ample time to wonder about Joseph Templeton as she lay awake that night. Ollie's explanation had been reasonable enough, and it was borne upon her quite forcibly that she knew very little about her mother's family. As far as she could tell, the likeness of Harriet Clifford portrayed in her locket bore no resemblance to the man she had seen that day. Of course, the painter may have used artistic licence with his palette, but the young woman whose features her daughter had gazed upon so many times had blond hair. Surely, had it been red… That the gentleman she had seen might be Clifford kin she dismissed immediately. For a start, she had many times seen the family tree, of which her father was so proud. They may have fallen upon hard times, but their line was unimpeachable. Of course, it could have been that the black sheep's name had been expunged from the record. It wouldn't be the first time such a thing had been done. But no, it just didn't feel right. Whatever his origins, Joseph Templeton wasn't a Clifford.

It wasn't until two days later when Elizabeth was trying for the third time to gain Sophie's attention that the matter was brought into the open.

"You seem distracted, my dear. Is something troubling you?"

They were seated in the dining room, Sophie abstractedly holding her fork but making no movement, when she realised she was being addressed. Alert once more, she replied, "No, of course not. Well, that isn't entirely true. There is one thing that has been taxing my mind for a while now. You may recall that I came home early on Tuesday, Lord Bridlington being kind enough to escort me. I didn't mention it at the time, but we encountered a gentleman that day whose appearance disturbed me." She paused, smiling a little sheepishly. "You see, he had red hair. Like mine. Oliver said something about families and skeletons, but I cannot deny it has disturbed me."

Elizabeth glanced quickly at her son as though questioning how to proceed but Rufus, though he would not unasked have imparted any information on the subject, decided that if Sophie was troubled it was time she learned the truth. Better from them than some stranger.

"I believe I can enlighten, though you may not like what you are about to hear."

She tried to laugh it off. "What, is there a murderer in my past?"

"Nothing as dramatic as that, I assure you. It is thought that Templeton is your father."

"What!"

"Forgive me, before you were born it was all about town that your mother and Templeton were, well, that there was a liaison between them. Her marriage to Clifford was not a love match. He was hanging out for a rich bride and she was a very wealthy young woman. Her parents wanted the title, of course, and pushed her into an alliance not of her own choosing. And in any case she was already enamoured of Templeton. Charming. Flamboyant. Childhood friends, they had reached maturity and had fallen in love. It was the talk of the town at the time. And later, forgive me, she died and you were never seen and the ton found something else to gossip about."

"But my father. Clifford, I mean. He took me as his own. Why?"

"The money, of course."

"No wonder he has always shown me so little affection. And has kept me cooped up at Charnwood." Sophie rose and paced about the room in agitation. "And Francis! His persistence in pursuing me. His veiled comments. This explains everything!" she said, the tremble in her voice impossible to hide. She sat down once more and folded her hands in her lap with tightly gripped fingers. And with an attempt at humour she said, "It is hardly surprising he deems himself such a catch. I gather then that I am ruined."

It took a while for Sophie to assimilate what she had learned but, strangely enough, instead of being subjected to gloom by the revelation of her true parentage, she was in better spirits than ever.

"You cannot understand what a relief it is to me to know that my mother and father truly loved each other," she said later to Lydia, who had been apprised of the situation. "Far better that I was born from them than a cold-hearted man whose ambition was to use me for his own ends."

"But this could spell the end of any hope you have of making a happy marriage."

"Yes, and obviously that's what Francis kept alluding to, though of course I didn't understand why at the time. If Society shuns me, well, I am a wealthy woman and will set up with Bertha to bear me company."

"Are you mad? Do you not care what people will say about you?"

"I am not so brazen as to be indifferent. Of course I'm not. But don't you see?" Sophie took her friend's hands into her own and fixed her eyes upon her. "They will talk anyway, whichever path I follow."

There could be no doubting the truth of this statement, but Lydia could not see it as a satisfactory solution. She suggested they talk to Elizabeth, saying that her mother was a woman of uncommon good sense and would no doubt come up with a wiser suggestion than younger heads could muster.

"I must indeed talk to your mother, for she may desire that I leave immediately. I would not wish to embarrass her by staying longer than I am welcome, particularly when she has been so kind to me. Anyway, I am pleased to know the truth. At least I now understand the occasional sideways glances where before I feared a smudge on my nose or some other such blemish."

Realistically, though, she comprehended that her future would be far different from anything she had until now envisaged. She couldn't help but be sad. These last few months had been the best of her life and had shown her an existence never before experienced. Well, she must cherish what she'd had and move on, for nothing was more certain in her mind than that she could no longer impose on the hospitality of her hosts.

Sophie had no clear idea as to what her next move might be. She knew only that she would be mortified beyond bearing if she were to be the cause of any discomfort in the Solgrave household. It was Lydia's first Season, and no risk must be run that might reflect upon her. Consequently, it was with a determination that paid no small tribute to her character that she told Elizabeth she would be leaving in the near future. If necessary, she would remove to a hotel.

"You cannot have considered, my dear. If your aim is to save me embarrassment, which I do not accept for one moment would be the case, how do you think it would appear if you left the shelter of Grosvenor Square to stay in such an alternative accommodation?"

Sophie had to admit this aspect had not occurred to her, and she realised that Lydia had spoken the truth when she talked about her mother's common sense. But she would not be turned from her decision.

"If that would be inappropriate, and I can see why it might be, I shall find another solution. But be sure, my dear friend, that one way or another I will stand on my own two feet. I can only be grateful that you have put up with me for so long, for you have been generous indeed, giving me your time and aid when your total focus might be expected to have been upon your daughter."

"Nonsense. I have such a fondness for you that I regard you almost as another daughter."

Nothing was going to deflect Sophie from her decision, but this last brought a constriction to her throat and she found it necessary to turn away for a moment in an attempt to conceal her emotions. Lady Luxton tried another approach.

"In any case, nothing has changed. Only that you are now aware of the circumstances."

"But don't you see, Elizabeth? Everything has changed because I am aware."

It was evident to her hostess that Sophie was in a high state of agitation and that, for the time being, nothing would be gained by continuing the conversation. She merely added, "All I would ask is that you do nothing in haste. You could do more harm than good, and the situation is not urgent. We have been going along quite nicely, besides which we are committed to several social engagements in the next few weeks. Think how it would appear if you were not to attend with me and Lydia as arranged. Such behaviour could spell ruin for you and, you will forgive me, would reflect extremely badly upon me. No, I insist, even if you don't accept any more such invitations, that you remain until those in place are fulfilled."

There was an inescapable logic with which Sophie could not argue, but she insisted that she would leave as soon as her obligations were discharged. For the time being, Elizabeth had to be content with that.

It seemed to Sophie that Joseph Templeton's return to London after such a long absence had already been noted by a few. There was no discernible change that the Luxtons could detect, but she was sure of it. Perhaps it was that she was solicited for fewer dances or that her opinion was not so readily sought in general conversation. No-one gave her the cut direct and, had she not been aware of the alteration in her circumstances, she would probably not have noticed anything amiss. One evening, at a soirée given by a long-standing friend of the countess, Rufus and Ollie were standing a little apart, watching a group that included Luxton's mother, his sister and Miss Clifford. He thought she seemed a little tense and knew the situation weighed heavily upon her.

"She's determined to go, Ollie, though I think as yet she has no specific plan. My mother is certain there would be no reflection upon Lydia, were she to remain, but she will not hear of it."

Bridlington was well aware of all that had transpired after he'd escorted Sophie home that first time she'd seen her father. She had herself thanked him for his consideration and, though he made light of it, he too was troubled. A smile slowly dawned upon his face and he turned from the ladies to his friend. "It may be that I have a way to resolve the problem. I shall say no more now, for it involves someone else, but don't be surprised if Miss Clifford leaves Grosvenor Square even sooner than any of you had anticipated." No further information could be elicited from him, but it was not many days later that Rufus had cause to congratulate his friend on his strategy. Bridlington was once more walking with Sophie in Hyde Park, an occupation both enjoyed and frequently indulged. At the approach of a carriage, Ollie waved and it drew to a halt beside them.

"Good morning, Mama. It's a fine day and nice to see you taking the air once again. May I make known to you Miss Sophie Clifford? Miss Clifford, my mother, Lady Bridlington."

"Won't you join me, Miss Clifford? Craning my neck does little for my aches and pains, and we will be much more comfortable if you climb into my carriage."

Sophie did so and found herself face to face with a formidable-looking dowager. A small woman, she was as neat as a pin and, it soon became plain, as sharp as a needle.

"I will not lie to you, my dear. Oliver has told me much about you and it is no accident that we meet today. You will forgive my son for making your circumstances known to me. In the light of what he has said, there will soon be many others cognisant of your situation."

Sophie liked Lady Bridlington immediately. This was not somebody who would beat about the bush, and she was grateful not to have the need to dissemble. "In that case, it is undeniably kind of you to take me up."

"We will take a turn around the park so that all and sundry may observe us. That'll show 'em." Sophie thought her delightful. "And while we do," she continued, "we shall discuss how to go forward. I doubt if Oliver has spoken much of his mother. You young people have far more interesting things to discuss. My husband died many years ago and I reside in lonely splendour in a rather large house in Berkeley Square." Not for one moment did her companion believe this redoubtable woman was lonely. She was therefore quite shocked at what came next. "I should like you to join me there as my companion."

"I beg your pardon? I mean, excuse me, but I don't understand."

"Nonsense. There is nothing amiss with your intellect. I could see that from the start. I am not exaggerating when I say I am a respected member of Society. So too is Lady Luxton, and she is a particular friend of mine. You will appreciate that we move in the same circles. The only reason I have not met you before today is because I have, for the past few weeks, been laid low with one of those ailments that so often afflict people of my age." Sophie was amazed any such ailment would dare to impose itself on this lady. "Miss Clifford, I will be frank with you. I have been told of your wish to leave the protection of the Luxtons for fear your presence there might have an adverse effect on the prospects of Miss Solgrave. I have to tell you that I admire those sentiments, and it may be there is some truth in your suspicions. If you come to live with me, you will have no such considerations. You will continue to attend such functions as you receive invitations for, and you will find that before long this will all have blown over and there will be some much larger scandal to take its place."

"It's very kind of you, Lady Bridlington, but I couldn't possibly."

"Don't be missish, child. It don't suit you. And there's Oliver waiting for us. Down you get now, and I shall expect you in Berkeley Square by the end of the week." She smiled and laid a hand on Sophie's arm. "Don't worry, my dear. I am certain you and I will get along famously."

The carriage drew to a halt, Sophie alighted and the equipage pulled away, leaving her to stare after it and wonder if what she thought had happened truly had. But there was a bubble of mirth inside her. She liked Lady Bridlington. She liked her very much.

CHAPTER EIGHT

Before moving in, and with Elizabeth as her escort, Sophie had twice visited Berkeley Square and found Lady Bridlington to be as delightful a companion as her son. Ollie had become a firm friend and she felt entirely at ease with him. And it was to him that she imparted the information that her fears had been well-founded.

"I cannot ignore it any longer, Oliver. On two occasions I have found new acquaintances, previously perfectly amenable, passing me by with their heads averted. I could not doubt."

Usually a jovial chap, Oliver had a serious side which he chose for the most part to keep hidden. It came now to the fore as he said, "I do not question you. You are a level-headed woman who, I think, would not confuse imaginings with reality. Why do you think this is happening only now?"

"You must remember that Joseph Templeton came only recently to London. It may be that he is out and about more and people are conjuring up memories of a rumour they heard twenty-one years ago. Anyone who has encountered us both could be in little doubt, I think. Our hair-colouring is unusual and distinctive enough to dispel any ambiguity."

"Have you seen him again?"

"I haven't, but others may well have done so."

"Then I fear there is little you can do other than brazen it out. My mother will support you, I know."

"I only hope she will not have cause to regret her invitation."

Ollie's mood reverted immediately to what she was used to seeing in him as he laughed aloud. "Not her! She loves a challenge. I'd give much to be present if anyone dares say anything to her on the subject."

"That's all very well," Sophie said, her own eyes alight with laughter, "but I would prefer it not to be so."

He became serious once again. A young woman in Sophie's position could not speak out and defend herself. And against what? Hers had not been the sin. She could only pretend things were as normal, and hope she continued to receive invitations in spite of the gossip.

Over the next few weeks, there was indeed a decline in the number of cards that were brought to the door. To say Sophie pined would have been a gross exaggeration, for solicitations still came in sufficient numbers for her only to have to remain at home if she chose to do so, but there was a marked difference in the treatment she received from some who had previously been so welcoming towards her.

It was when she was riding Snowflake in the park one day that Sophie once again encountered the man she now knew to be her father. He was coming from the opposite direction and she had ample time to see him properly as he approached, for they were this time on the same level. There was no slowing of pace as he drew near, and she realised it was his intention to pass straight by. But why? For her protection? Or was it because he had no desire to acknowledge her? She could not know, but, more than anything in the world, she wanted to meet him. Whether or not he might want to meet her she could only conjecture. Her companion was Rufus Solgrave, and she whispered hastily, "I'd like to stop."

"By all means. I think it a right decision."

They drew to a halt just as Templeton came alongside them. Luxton raised a hand in greeting and Sophie smiled, while at the same time holding her breath. What if he gave her the go by? He did not, and she was as sure as she could be that he was glad to have it so. It was Rufus who eased the tension by saying, "Joseph Templeton, I believe. Forgive us for addressing you, but Miss Clifford here has expressed a desire to meet you. Allow me to introduce myself. I am Luxton."

"Good day to you, Lord Luxton. Miss Clifford," he said, turning to face Sophie for the first time. She could see pain in his eyes, and relief and, she thought, something approaching hope. "You cannot have wished for this meeting more than I. I would not have… But this is not the place. I am aware you are at present residing in Berkeley Square, but naturally I cannot visit you at Lady Bridlington's home. Luxton," he said, turning to the other man, "I wonder, should I give you my direction, if you might perhaps find a way for me to meet … my daughter."

There! The words were out. They could not be unsaid. And in that moment a bond was forged.

Over the following days Sophie was shunned and courted in almost equal measure. She had the satisfaction of knowing that there was never a dance she was obliged to sit out. But she was no fool. She was well aware that she was in possession of a large fortune which acted as a magnet to those gentlemen in search of a wealthy wife. She judged the attention she received to be shallow but was grateful for it nonetheless. Not for her the ignominy of sitting by the wall at parties for want of a partner. Her experience with Francis Follet had taught her that there are many things an impecunious man about town might ignore when in desperate straits.

Fortunately, Luxton, Bridlington and Conroy treated her the same as ever and they could not know what comfort she derived, knowing that it was so. They had no ulterior motive for seeking her out, she was certain. If they maintained their by now habitual association with her, it was because they enjoyed her company.

Conroy's affection for Lydia could be seen to be growing day by day and, though he never overstepped the mark, it was evident where his hopes lay. Oliver Bridlington was a man with no side, his behaviour as ever like that of an older brother. But Sophie would have been surprised to learn that Luxton was not indifferent to her. Rufus, though she was no longer under his mother's protection and living in his house, was unsure enough of his feelings as to make any change in his attitude towards her unnoticeable. No youth was he, to have his head turned by a beautiful face, but he was unfamiliar with the emotions that prompted him to shelter Sophie from pain or discomfort. Until such time as he could determine his own sentiments, he would not compromise hers. One thing he knew. He was missing her daily presence in Solgrave House and feeling a pang of envy that Oliver saw more of her than he could now do. Bridlington's mother resided permanently at the house in Berkeley Square and, while her son was frequently absent from town, either on some jaunt or at his family seat, it was still his base when in London and, for the time being at least, he was going nowhere.

Visiting Elizabeth Solgrave one morning when her daughter was out walking with friends, Sophie remarked, "You cannot have failed to notice, I am sure, that there are those of your acquaintance who do not approach you when we are together. It can only confirm to me that my decision to leave Grosvenor Square was a right one. Not for the world would I have Lydia suffer because of our connection."

"I would be less than truthful if I denied what you are saying, and I can only declare that I will be more careful in the future when choosing my friends."

"No, do not say so. It is the way of the world and a sad reflection upon how Society judges people but, conversely, it is not for us to judge them. I merely wanted you to know that I will never forget what you have done these past months. It is fortunate for me that Lady Bridlington has no daughter to protect from a slur by association."

"You are in good hands, that much is certain. She may be small of stature but Augusta most definitely lives up to her name, and I have never yet seen anyone get the better of her."

"Yes, indeed." Sophie paused before adding, almost as if constrained to do so, "This may strike you as an odd thing to say, but I will forever be grateful for the day I was knocked off my horse. Had your son not been kind enough to rescue me and carry me back to Ashby, I might still be residing in misery at Charnwood."

"Was it so bad?" Elizabeth leaned forward and placed a hand on her arm, a gesture of sympathy for which an unusually subdued Sophie was grateful.

"At the time I don't think I was aware of it. Well, perhaps I was, but to a much lesser degree. It had always been so. I knew no different. It was a loveless home. Oh, I know that my step-mama dotes on her odious son, but there was no affection in her dealings with me. And now, of course, I understand why, and I know why my father was so cold towards me."

As she finished speaking, Elizabeth removed her hand and Sophie rose and took a turn about the room. Her discomposure was evident, her stride not the controlled pace of a young lady. Lady Luxton did not seek to stop her, knowing she needed these moments to reflect on her sadness and vent her frustration. The pacing ceased abruptly and Sophie returned to her seat, the bleak look leaving her eyes as she pushed away memories which Elizabeth could only imagine.

"What a harridan you must think me. I must beg your forgiveness. How rude of me to inflict my ill temper upon you."

"Don't think it. Sometimes it is helpful to give expression to what is within one's heart. Now, let me ring for tea and we shall talk about something less distressing. Do you go to the Fortescues' soirée tomorrow?"

Sophie was riding with Bridlington the next morning, Snowflake having been transferred from Luxton's stables to his own, when they were waylaid by Rufus himself.

"I would speak with you urgently, Miss Clifford. You too, Oliver. Do you return to Berkeley Square after your ride? I will join you there."

He then took his leave of them and Ollie said, "It is unlike Rufus to be enigmatic. I wonder what he wants."

"Certainly he seemed to have something on his mind. Would you object too much if we curtailed our ride this morning, Lord Bridlington? I don't know about you, but I detected some urgency in Lord Luxton's manner. He will not be long in joining us, I think."

She was proved right when Solgrave arrived in Berkeley Square only half an hour behind them. They were by this time seated with Lady Bridlington, who was protesting in a teasing way that she had missed her carriage ride that day and hoped Miss Clifford would join her on the morrow. "I had forgotten how much I enjoyed the pastime, though I must say that most of my pleasure is derived from watching my fellows rather than admiring the scenery."

"And I have deprived you of that pleasure, ma'am. Forgive me. I shall make reparations as soon as I may. In the meantime, will you allow me to fetch your shawl? It is a little chillier today, I think."

She rose and was about to leave the room when Lord Luxton was announced. She glanced up at him before excusing herself with a smile that caused his heart to thump. Returning swiftly, Sophie wrapped the garment about Augusta's shoulders before seating herself once more and looking enquiringly at Rufus. "You have something pressing to say, I understand?"

"It is of a somewhat private nature. Forgive me, Lady Bridlington," he said, throwing her a smile so sweet that she could not be offended when he said, "Would you mind excusing us?"

But it was Sophie who replied. "My circumstances are known to all of us here. I would not exclude anyone if you have come to tell me what I believe to be the purpose of your call."

"Then I must tell you that I have been in contact with Joseph Templeton and arranged to meet him tomorrow at midday, at an inn I know of in Barnet. He is waiting even now for me to confirm that you are able to come with me."

She stared at him. Her fingers pleated and unpleated the muslin of her gown before she composed herself again. "You said, I know, that you would arrange a meeting, so you may wonder why I appear to be surprised. The truth is that I cannot believe this is actually happening. Of course I will come."

"You too, Oliver, if you would. I want no whisper of scandal attached to Miss Clifford's name, and it is preferable that we both escort her."

"It will be a pleasure."

"Then it only remains for me to confirm with Templeton. I will call for you at ten o'clock."

He rose and took his leave, Lady Bridlington remarking, "Ah well, it would seem my own carriage ride will have to wait." But she was smiling, and Sophie ran over to her and dropped to the floor beside her. She took Augusta's hands in her own.

"You are the best of people. I cannot thank you enough."

As the day progressed, it became apparent that Sophie was on tenterhooks. Lady Bridlington was of the opinion that activity was the answer to most problems.

"I have had it in mind for a while now to replace the ribbons on my straw bonnet. They are sadly crumpled and I cannot achieve a desirable bow when I tie them under my chin. It is time to visit the milliner."

Sophie felt the last thing she wanted to do was to go shopping, but naturally she acquiesced and was surprised at how much she enjoyed the experience. The proprietor was no fool. She attended first to Lady Bridlington, persuading her that it was not only the ribbons that had seen better days. A new straw bonnet was purchased along with two caps. She was able then to turn her attention to the younger woman, a dream customer. Sophie's beauty and colouring meant that every cap or bonnet that was placed upon her head showed to advantage. An hour later the ladies left the establishment, both well satisfied. Even more so the milliner, who was not crude enough to ask that they mention her to their acquaintance. She knew well that those who admired Sophie's hats would enquire as to where they had been purchased.

They were engaged to go to a soirée that evening. Sophie was delighted to see that Elizabeth and Lydia were both present and she moved to greet them. She had just sat down when she observed Mrs Vaughan coming towards them. As she looked up, the woman stopped in her tracks and turned away. There could be no doubt as to why she had changed her mind. All Sophie's pleasure was gone and even though Lady Luxton, who had also observed the slight, tried to reassure her, she could not be soothed. Angry tears sprung to her eyes but she dashed them away under cover of her fan.

"You must excuse me. I would not for the world have caused you embarrassment." She rose and returned to Lady Bridlington, moving gracefully and without hurry, determined that Mrs Vaughan should not have the satisfaction of knowing how discomfited she was.

"Well done, my dear. I must say you handled that with more class than that dreadful woman showed," Augusta said, having watched the whole scene from her chair on the other side of the room.

"If you don't object, I should like to go home."

"Absolutely not! You cannot run away now. You must show the world you are not confounded. To leave now would be to acknowledge something is wrong. Be brave for a while longer, my dear."

And so it was that Sophie fell gratefully into bed some hours later. Anticipation of tomorrow and the happenings of the evening had drained her so much that she fell into a deep and dreamless sleep.

CHAPTER NINE

The drizzle that greeted Sophie's eyes when Bertha drew back the curtains the next morning was not sufficient to quell her excitement. Gone was the despair of the night before. Today she would meet her father, and she was certain she had much to learn from him. She dressed with care and, when the time came to go, she donned a full-length tan pelisse trimmed with swansdown and one of the new bonnets she had purchased the previous afternoon. It gave her an added lift, knowing she looked well.

Taking leave of her hostess, she went with Oliver to the waiting carriage. Striving for anonymity, Rufus had hired a coach and driver to take them to Barnet. As they came near Sophie's excitement grew, but so also did her apprehension. *What if I am a disappointment to him?* she wondered. Clutching her reticule tightly, she alighted and went into the inn, Luxton showing the way and Bridlington at her elbow. The landlord directed them to a private room and departed. As they entered, Joseph Templeton turned towards them from where he was standing by the window. The other two men stood aside and father and daughter joined in the middle of the salon, hand to hand and eye to eye. It was uncertain as to whether or not either heard Rufus say, "We will leave you now. Should you need us, we'll be in the taproom."

"You have my colouring, but you have the look of your mother," Templeton said, the wonderment evident in his voice. He stood back from her, the better to see. "So you are my child. There can be no doubt. But what am I thinking? Sit down. Refresh yourself, for we have much to discuss."

Sophie responded as one in a daze and, removing her pelisse and bonnet, accepted the proffered glass. He sat beside her and it seemed they could not drag their eyes away from one another.

"I know only a little of the story, and that but recently. I have always believed the baron to be my father and sometimes wondered why he showed me so little affection. Well, now I know. But wait. You say I resemble my mother. Is this not then she?" Sophie asked, unfastening her locket and handing it to him. He opened it and she could see how he struggled with his emotions.

"It is your mother, but it's not a good likeness. I can see how you would not perceive the similarities between you. They are of a subtle nature. How I have longed these many years to look upon her face." He closed the locket reluctantly and handed it back to her, but she held up her hand.

"I have worn this all my life, but it is of someone I never knew. Keep it, for I can see how much it means to you. But tell me the whole story, if you please, for thus far I have only hearsay."

Unconsciously he played with the locket as she watched him reach into his past to relate what had really happened all those years ago. "I met Harriet Clifford, or Harriet Munro as she then was, when we were just children, for our estates marched side by side. Every day she would ride her pony and I would wait for her at the five bar gate. Imagine, if you will, two children growing as friends to adulthood and then falling in love. Only I wasn't an acceptable suitor for the Munros."

"You carried neither wealth nor title?"

"Oh, I had an adequate fortune, or the prospect of one, my father still being alive at the time. But it wasn't riches your ambitious grandfather was after. He had sufficient wealth of his own. No, what he had was an aspiration to raise himself within Society, and he used his only daughter to achieve his aims." He spoke with a long-standing bitterness and with an effort composed himself before continuing. "I begged and pleaded with him, but a plain Mister was not good enough. Harriet was not proof against his bullying and she was lost to me from the moment Clifford offered for her." He paused and looked at the locket in his hands, opening it once more. "I shall wear this, if you have no objection. No-one will see it beneath my clothes and Harriet will be next to my heart, though the truth is she has always been there."

"And the wedding?" Sophie asked, wanting him to continue.

"She was barely seventeen. She tried to be a good wife, but she was so desperately unhappy. Somehow we managed to see each other, in secret we thought, but there were those who suspected. And then one day, God forgive me, my feelings overcame me. And you, my darling daughter, are the product of our union. When I learned that Harriet was expecting, I didn't know whether to feel elated or desperate. You see, I had no idea if the child she was carrying was mine or her husband's."

He paused and walked to the window, overcome for a while and unable to go on. Sophie poured another drink for each of them and waited with as much patience as she could muster. After some moments, he returned to his chair and continued with his story.

"You will understand, Sophie, that when your mother was confined there was no way I could see her. And then I heard that she had not survived childbirth. I have never known such grief. Forgive me, but I had no thought for the baby. I was convinced it was Clifford's child. After all, it had only been that once that we…" He looked at her directly. "What chance that you were mine? I left England almost immediately and have returned only for short visits, but my father died recently and I came back to take my place as head of the family."

"And have you never married?"

"There was never anyone else. Can you imagine my joy when I learned that I had a child? But my delight turned to concern when I realised the ramifications that knowledge might have for you."

"I care not for such things."

"Then I must care for you. It is hard enough being a man in the world and alone. It is a fate I wouldn't wish upon anyone, and certainly not a woman." He paused and breathed in deeply before continuing, "I would see you again, if you are willing, but we must be discreet. I have been absent your whole life and unable to care for you as a father should. Allow me to know better how cruel the world can be and, if I can, to protect you from such cruelty."

"Papa. I may call you Papa? I will not let you go now that I have found you, for I too have led a lonely life. But, yes, if it pleases you I will be guided by your discretion."

"Then it is time we called your escorts back. I will liaise with Luxton on when and how we can meet again."

He moved to the door and opened it at the very moment Mr and Mrs Vaughan entered the inn. She glanced over in his direction and from her surprised expression it was evident that Sophie was plainly to be seen in the room behind him. Mrs Vaughan stopped so abruptly that her unfortunate spouse, following behind, walked straight into her. As she turned to admonish him, Templeton stepped back inside and closed the door, but it was too late. He knew they had been spotted, and by someone whose reputation left him in no doubt that she would show no compassion, either for him or his daughter.

Moments later there was a gentle knock on the door. Rufus and Oliver entered. From their position in the taproom they had observed what had happened.

"Now the cat is truly set among the pigeons," Oliver remarked. "She is the very last person we might expect to behave with discretion. We must take you home, Miss Clifford, and decide how to move forward from this misfortune."

"You are, all of you, determined to protect me and I want you to know that I appreciate your concern. But the sky has not yet fallen and I have been lucky enough after all these years to know who my true parent is. A man who can tell me about my mother, things that no-one else ever has because she was never discussed." She looked at Templeton. "I was used to thinking it was because of my father's grief. I know now that it wasn't the case. But you, you have grieved half a lifetime. I would know more of the woman whose image I have carried all these years in my locket. We will meet again. And, if I am to be ostracised, so be it."

"You don't know what you're saying, my child. This could ruin you."

Sophie stood proudly before them and not one doubted her resolution when she said, "Society may have chosen to damn my parents for their wrongdoing. It is, I know, the way of the world. If I too must be damned, then it is a society I would not wish to be part of. I'm not a fool, but London is not the world. If necessary I will remove to the country, to some quiet place where nobody knows me. What I will not do is give up something I have yearned for all my life. The love of a parent."

"I applaud you for your courage, Miss Clifford," said Rufus, "but I fear you are in for a rough time. You will have support from my family, and Oliver's too, I know. Let us not anticipate what is to come but, whatever that may be, it will be my honour to face it with you."

"That's the ticket, Luxton. We'll see this through together," agreed Oliver.

"I cannot allow either of you, or your families, to risk your own reputations on my behalf."

"Pooh! I lost my own years ago, and my mother won't give a hoot what other people say. What did you think, Luxton? A bit like our old campaigning days, eh?"

"Not quite, Ollie, but I admire your sentiments. And I echo them. Let me just check to see if that awful woman has left, for it is time we returned to Berkeley Square. Templeton, I shall be in touch. Allow me to say it has been a pleasure."

"And may I say thank you. You have given me a cherished treasure."

He remained in the room and, as they left, his daughter turned to look at him once more. He did not see. His head was lowered as he gazed once more upon the image of the woman he had loved and lost. Never had Sophie given so valuable a gift.

In very little time it became evident that the worst predictions of Sophie's protectors were realised. Only determined fortune-hunters solicited her hand for a dance or paid morning calls to the house in Berkeley Square. Invitations no longer came or, if they did, they were for Lady Bridlington alone and were to a card evening or some such small affair with her friends. Sophie was a proud young woman but she could not dismiss the hurt, for what, after all, had she done? *If people choose not to recognise me, so be it*, she thought, her chin raised in defiance. The solution she had envisaged at the inn was still an option, and one that was appealing to some extent, but she had come to realise that she enjoyed life in the capital. The theatre, which she was still able to attend; dancing, where now she was constrained to sitting on the side of the room watching others; the very superior shops where she took pleasure in indulging herself. One thing was certain. She would never return to Charnwood!

"I cannot tell you how disappointed I am in a number of my acquaintance whom I have previously called friend. To be swayed by the judgement of such a person as Mrs Vaughan, who has less refinement in her little finger than you have in your whole body."

Sophie laughed at Elizabeth Solgrave, who had come with Lydia to Berkeley Square, and thanked her for the compliment, but she protested too. "Though I cannot sufficiently express my delight in seeing you both, I must ask that you do not call again. If I thought for one moment that Lydia might be tainted by association, I would be mortified beyond anything."

"Well, you need not worry about Lydia's reputation. It is not generally known yet, and I beg you will say nothing until the official announcement, but I am sure it will come as no surprise to you that my lovely daughter has received an offer of marriage from Frederick Conroy."

"I wanted you to be the first to know, for you are my best of friends, Sophie. And I would ask that you stand with me in attendance at the ceremony."

Sophie hugged Lydia and then Lady Luxton. "I could not be happier for you." She paused, for what she had to say next would not, she knew, be well-received. "You will understand, however, that I must decline your invitation. It does not follow that because you are to be married you are safe from criticism. I will not be the cause. I ask nothing more than to sit quietly and unobtrusively in the church when you make your vows."

Both mother and daughter began to protest, but it was Lady Bridlington who intervened and said, "I'm afraid Sophie is right. The implications of this dreadful situation will, I trust, subside with time, but that time has not yet come. She will remain with me and we will sit it out together. We are not devoid of company, for there are some who are true to me and others who have more sense than to blame her for her birth. There is much we can do. Her daily ride in the park. Our outings in my carriage. Visits to Drury Lane. We shall do."

"No, Lady Bridlington, I'm afraid we shall not do," Sophie said. Her voice rang with determination, but there was a desolate look in her eyes. "I cannot remain here. In spite of what you say, there are consequences for you as well. You have been kind to me beyond anything I could have asked. Both of you have. But it is time I made my own way. I have engaged an agent to find a suitable house for me to hire and will remove there as soon as matters have been arranged. Bertha will come with me and I shall find an appropriate lady to act as my companion for, under the circumstances, I cannot entirely fly in the face of convention. Then, if my father wishes, he may visit me without the necessity of finding out of the way places to meet. It breaks my heart that each time he sees me he looks constantly around to determine whether or not we are being watched. This has happened twice already, and it is not how I want to carry on."

It was a long speech and it reduced her listeners to silence, Lydia with tears running down her cheeks and the other two with such a sadness that Sophie was hard put herself not to cry. They did not argue. It would, they knew, have been fruitless. Her hostess said simply, "I have grown to enjoy your company. I shall miss you."

"And now, before you leave, tell me all about the wedding, Lydia. When is it to be? Have you chosen your bridal gown? You have chosen a very handsome husband, to be sure."

The tension was lifted and the atmosphere lightened immediately. Certain things had already been decided. An announcement of the betrothal was to be sent to the *Morning Post* the very next day. Her tears forgotten, Miss Solgrave could not conceal her excitement, and it was a much happier group who said their goodbyes an hour later. Only then did Sophie excuse herself and, in the privacy of her own room, permit herself to give vent to her true feelings.

The agent had served Sophie well and she moved into her new accommodation in Hay Hill, not far from where she had been staying with Lady Bridlington in Berkeley Square. It was perhaps a little on the large side for a single occupant and her companion, but it was a good address and she could afford to be extravagant. It came furnished, "which is just as well," she confided to Luxton when he came to see her, "for the task of equipping a house of this size would be a challenge I would not wish to undertake at this point, though there are some changes I intend to make so that it serves me better."

He looked around with interest. "If I may be permitted to say so, the hangings and chair covers in this room have been chosen with good taste. Their colour is similar, I believe, to that of your riding habit and you have remarked that it is a favourite of yours."

"It certainly is," she said, smiling because she was rather pleased that he had noticed.

"Then you are fortunate to find it here. I cannot say I admire that overly large painting above the fireplace. It doesn't suit the room, or you, at all."

"And what, sir, if I thought it a wonderful piece of artwork that enhanced its surroundings?" she said, her smile broadening to a grin. "I might have been grossly offended."

He laughed aloud. "Not you. I credit you with far better judgement. In fact, I am amazed to see it at all. Would you like me to have it taken down?"

"No, for I have nothing yet to replace it and it will have left a mark on the wall. I agree, though. It's hideous."

Finding a suitable companion had not been quite as easy as finding a house, and had it not been for Rufus coming to her aid she might still be searching.

"I cannot thank you enough for your help. Emily is a charming girl, and we rub along together very well. I admit to having suffered a degree of guilt in taking your cousin away from her parents, but my understanding now is that she was dreadfully put upon and almost as unhappy as I had been at Charnwood. Once I knew that, my reservations evaporated."

"I imagine we all have relations with whom we are not best pleased to associate. Emily's parents are not my sort of people. Does that sound arrogant? I fear it must, but Miss Bracken is not like them and I have always felt some compassion for her. It is you who do her the favour, Miss Clifford, not the other way around."

"Well, that's fustian, I'm sure. But she has some spirit, which I like, and she doesn't rattle on but can conduct a sensible conversation."

All at once, and to Sophie's surprise, Rufus was suddenly angry, something she was able to discern if not from his words then certainly from the tone in which he uttered them. "And she is now conspicuous by her absence. What purpose then does she serve? How would it be if you received another visitor while alone with me in this room? You have sought to protect the reputation of others by setting up on your own. Have you no thought for yourself?"

Flushed cheeks were witness to her own indignation. "I am beholden to you for many reasons, sir, but I will not have you dictate my conduct. Emily is at present lying on her bed with the headache."

"In which case you should have had your footman decline to announce me."

"I have regarded you as a friend. It would never have occurred to me to turn you away merely because of what others might construe. How can you think so?"

"It seems one of us must think." Rufus paced the room in an effort to get his temper under control. Speaking more calmly but with no less feeling, he said, "You have spent a lifetime confined to one small corner of Buckinghamshire. Unless you are adept at hiding your feelings, it has seemed to me that you have embraced the opportunities London has to offer. You are in a precarious position. Some but not all of your acquaintance have withdrawn from you. Whatever, forgive me, might have been the actions of your mother and father, you do not in my opinion deserve that they should be laid at your door, but if you act in an irresponsible way now you will create your own boundaries as well as theirs. Do not underestimate how devastating the result of such actions might be."

Sophie jumped to her feet. "How dare you speak to me in this manner! You are neither my father nor my brother, and I will not accept criticism from you. I think perhaps it is time you left."

Rufus had come to the same conclusion but paused at the door. "I spoke not to criticise but to advise. If you continue in this way, I think you will find that the disapproval you may incur will have a far more detrimental effect upon your welfare. Please pay my respects to my cousin. I wish you good day."

Sophie looked at the closed door and could not help thinking it might be symbolic. She had allowed her pride to push her friend into an untenable position and now he had gone. Even had she been in an optimistic frame of mind, she must have concluded from his parting that it would be some considerable time before he called upon her again, if ever. She felt as if the ground had been torn from beneath her feet.

CHAPTER TEN

For the second time in only a few months, Sophie's existence underwent a sea change. She had been lonely all her life, but a different kind of loneliness descended upon her over the next few weeks. Conroy and Bridlington were frequent visitors, and she suspected they came as much out of compassion as from friendship. Rufus Solgrave she saw not at all. Elizabeth and Lydia stayed away at her request, but Lady Bridlington ignored her protests and often called her carriage to drive her the short distance to Hay Hill. These visits she was able to reciprocate with only a slight tinge of conscience, particularly when Augusta said, "I have attained an age where I may please myself above others, and it pleases me to spend time with you, Sophie. You may have chosen no longer to reside with me, but I am sure you would not offend an old lady by cutting our acquaintance entirely. You must yourself know what that feels like."

These visits served to help fill her days, but it was a different story when it came to the evenings. No longer did she find herself twirling around a ballroom or deep in discussion around the dinner table or in someone's drawing room. Those opportunities no longer presented themselves. Bridlington, aware of her love of theatre, organised two outings and she was able to enjoy them to their full extent but for one thing. On both occasions Lord Luxton had been present. He had exchanged greetings with her almost formally and taken his leave but had not otherwise sought her out, and she found she missed his company. Of all her new acquaintance, he had been the one with whom she had been most at ease, the one whose sense of humour so nearly matched hers.

"I had thought to see more of my cousin when I came to live with you," Emily said one afternoon when they were having tea. "My impression when he drove me here from my parents' home was that you and he were often in each other's company. Certainly you featured a great deal in his conversation."

If there was the hint of a question in Miss Bracken's voice, Sophie did not respond directly to it, merely saying that gentlemen led busy lives and one could never be sure when one might see them. Emily maintained her discretion, but what she thought would have given her employer much to speculate upon.

Following Luxton's last visit, Sophie had adhered to his advice and no longer received guests unless Emily too was present in the room. She wished only that she might have had an opportunity to tell him so. There was one exception to this rule. When Joseph Templeton called, Emily waited but a polite amount of time before excusing herself so that father and daughter could be alone. These were some of Sophie's happiest moments and, she considered, worth all the sorrow she was experiencing at other times. She had seen her father frequently enough now to feel able to question him, and she did this as they walked in the garden.

"You have described to me the circumstances of your leaving the country. Did you never seek to question whether or not the child my mother was carrying might be yours?"

"Of course I did, but you must understand. When you were born, well, I have already explained my grief. What I haven't told you is that one day, before I went away, I waylaid her maid when she was walking in the grounds of Charnwood. To my shame I had sneaked in unobserved. She told me that the babe, you, of course, was with a wet nurse. Kitty had been our ally in those few months of her marriage, and I knew I could trust her not to give me away."

"And was she able to tell you anything?"

"Only that you were, like so many babies, without any hair. Just bits of fluff, she said, that were perhaps a little brownish. Of your features, the only certain thing in her mind was that you looked so like Harriet that there was no scope for resemblance to another."

"And is that when you left?"

"No, I remained in England for a few weeks, but once Clifford accepted you as his own there seemed little reason to stay any longer. I felt sure, had there been any doubt, that he would have rejected you. That he didn't was sufficient to assure me that you were his child. And that was when I left. I never went back, so you can imagine my surprise when I saw you that day in the park. The image of Harriet but with my hair. Even under your riding hat I could see that much. It was one of the most joyful moments of my life, and little did I think then that it might be the ruin of you."

"You mustn't say that, Papa!"

Templeton came to a halt and turned to face her. "But it's true, don't you see? You are no longer welcomed in the best circles."

"Which is why they have ceased for me to be the best."

"Easy to say, Sophie, but in reality the world is a harsh place. I wish I had never come back. You could have lived your life without my shame hanging about you like a dark cloud."

Sophie gripped her father's hands and looked up into troubled eyes that were as green as her own. "I shall remain in London for this Season. I shall then remove to Buckinghamshire, where I will find a house in an area with which I am familiar. It is my dearest hope that you will visit me whenever you can. If by that time I am not accepted, I shall judge whether or not to return next year. In the meantime, there is nothing more important to me in the whole world than the love of my father. If there is a storm to come, we shall ride it together."

CHAPTER ELEVEN

A cool but sunny day in late February heralded the coming of spring. Sweeping shadows threw dramatic highlights across the aisle and pews in St George's Church in Hanover Square as friends and family gathered for the wedding of Lydia Solgrave and Freddie Conroy. Sophie sat out of the way as she had requested, Emily Bracken beside her. She watched wistfully as the bride was led by her brother to where the groom stood waiting. Her glimpses of Rufus had been few of late and she had to admit to herself that she missed his company, only she did not know how to mend the rift between them. She turned her attention to the happy couple and her heart warmed. As they took their vows and turned to face the assembled company, the pride on Freddie's face and the joy on Lydia's shone as brightly as the sunbeams which highlighted them.

Later, at the wedding breakfast, Lydia said, "I am so glad you came. It wouldn't have been the same without you, Sophie. And you are with friends here."

It was true. These people did not count amongst those who had rejected her and she was for the first time in a while able to hope that she might weather this storm and come out unscathed at the end of it. Augusta Bridlington said as much when the two had a few quiet moments together. "It is a pleasure to see you for once enjoying yourself. Be brave, my child. Your time will come." This was said in her usual forthright manner but with a squeeze of the hand. A prickling behind her eyelids made Sophie realise how lonely she had once more become, and she returned the other's pressure gratefully.

Emily was in conversation with her cousin nearby, close enough to turn to Sophie and say, "I have been telling Luxton once more how grateful I am for his efforts on my behalf. I have never been happier, and for that I have both of you to thank."

Rufus had no choice but to acknowledge Sophie. Emily, no fool, somehow managed to slip away.

"I have missed you." Sophie's words were uttered simply and straightforwardly.

Solgrave felt his gut wrench and realised that his anger had carried him so much further than was warranted. "I hope, in that case, that you will not turn me from your door should I come to visit," he said, a tentative smile accompanying his words.

Sophie's sense of humour, never far away, showed itself in a mischievous smile as she responded, "Of course not. I shall even ensure that Emily is with me."

"Miss Clifford, you are … incorrigible. I have not enjoyed this distancing between us. May I suggest we ride together in the park? I have passed you on many occasions and recall how much pleasure I took in our previous outings. Tomorrow, perhaps?"

"Snowflake and I will be delighted. Do not let me detain you. You have guests who are waiting to exchange greetings with you. I look forward to seeing you and pray this beautiful weather holds."

He moved away but in the space of those few minutes, Sophie's world had returned once again to an even keel.

The resumption of Sophie's rides with Rufus, combined with her walks with Oliver and the not infrequent excursions in his mother's carriage, served to create a much more normal pattern of existence. Where these two gentlemen went, and even more so Lady Bridlington, others went also. Not all others, it had to be said. She was still the object of exclusion and she could not deny the hurt. But she no longer left home in dread of not being acknowledged and, when it did happen, she went on by with her head held high.

Joseph Templeton had ceased to frequent the park, saying, "I would not be the cause of further unnecessary embarrassment. There are sufficient opportunities for me to leave my lodgings without my doing so and, now that I am able to visit you at home, there is no necessity for me to seek you out elsewhere."

Sophie had argued with him, asserting again that she had no time for those who would behave in so unmannerly a way. He let her know in no uncertain terms that she was being naïve and that sometimes pride goes before a fall. "Consider if you would, my child, how I would feel if our public association contributed to your discomfort. You will not move me in this instance. We are fortunate that we are able to meet on other occasions. Antagonising people unnecessarily will serve no purpose. We have discussed this enough. Tell me instead what invitations you have received of late."

They were seated in the morning room of her house in Hay Hill, and she rose to fetch a card from where it lay on a silver salver on the dresser. "I have only this one, newly arrived, but to my great astonishment the Sedgewicks have included me in the guest list for their forthcoming ball and have been kind enough to invite Emily to go with me."

"And why would they not? She comes, after all, from one of our most aristocratic families. But this is good news, Sophie. Perhaps the time has come for people to put aside their prejudice."

"I hope you are right. I will not be easy until I see how I am received but, as for Mr and Mrs Sedgewick, I cannot sufficiently express my gratitude."

In Emily, Sophie had found a friend. Her senior by a mere three years, they had much in common, perhaps the greatest difference being that Emily had expectation of only a small competence and was forced by circumstance to rely on the kindness of others, and to earn her own living. Once it was established that she was not to be treated like a paid servant but as an equal to her employer in all regards, any reservations either had entertained fell away.

"Forgive me, Emily, but may I ask, I wonder … there is no way to say it but the direct one. Do you have a ball gown?"

Emily laughed and assured Sophie she was in no way offended by the question. "I did once attend a ball, when I was not yet nineteen. What I wore was neither flattering nor would it be suitable for a woman of my age. Do not worry," she added, seeing the look of concern Sophie was unable to hide. "You pay me an exorbitant wage and I am perfectly able to purchase a new one. Whether or not there is sufficient time to find something that is both attractive and fits well enough not to require alteration is another question."

"As to that, I am sure there is nothing to fear. We shall engage the assistance of Lady Bridlington who will, I am certain, not only introduce us to the right establishment but also give her opinion. No, do not raise your eyebrows. She has the best taste of anyone and, if I know her, she will enjoy the outing immensely."

Sophie was nothing if not practical. The gown she had worn for Lydia's ball became her, and, with little idea as to when or even if she might receive another invitation, she concluded it would be more desirable to refurbish it than to purchase a new one. The dressmaker to whom Augusta took them was no fool. She raised no objection to carrying out alterations on a dress that was not of her own making. Lady Bridlington was a valued customer and Madame knew Miss Clifford to be a lady of some fortune. Treated tactfully, she would return. Miss Bracken too was a gift. Her trim figure and blond curls would suffice to set off one of her creations to the best advantage. She had a pale blue gown in mind and she and Augusta discussed it at some length when Emily stood before them, waiting for their verdict.

"Admirable, my dear, don't you think, Sophie?" Lady Bridlington asked.

"You look divine, Emily," Sophie agreed.

"Just a tuck here and there and it will fit you to perfection, Miss Bracken. Allow me to say what a pleasure it is to fit a young lady who shows to such advantage." She turned to Sophie. "Your own gown is quite beautiful, and I make my compliments to its designer," she said generously. "I think just a few changes here and there and we might create a look quite unexceptionable, and none will know they have seen it before."

"I give myself over to you entirely, Madame, and I thank you for agreeing to complete the work in so little time."

It being decided that new fans, reticules and other accessories were not only desirable but necessary, Lady Bridlington bore them off to the most fascinating emporium where they spent the rest of the day discovering unimagined delights and returned home with a much greater number of parcels than they had anticipated.

The day of the ball arrived, and as Bertha helped her into her gown Sophie could not help wondering with a little trepidation what was to come. Emily was hardly less anxious but, as the two stepped out of their carriage to enter the Sedgewicks' home, no-one could have been aware that each felt her heart was pounding in her ears.

Mr and Mrs Sedgewick were most gracious in their welcome of the two young ladies but, as they passed from the hall where greetings were being exchanged, their entrance to the ballroom created quite a stir. It was as if time stopped for a moment before the buzz of conversation resumed and they moved forward. Never had Sophie been so glad to see Elizabeth Solgrave, who was beckoning to her from the other side of the huge room. Her gaze took in outrageously ostentatious chandeliers, carvings on the high ceiling and walls, and three windows that went from coving to floor, all with double doors that could be opened onto the terrace. Through them she could see a multitude of candles flickering in sconces and illuminating the outside area, thus making it appear to be a continuation of the ballroom. As they approached, Elizabeth rose in greeting and begged them to join her. "With Lydia and Freddie away on their honeymoon, I am sorely in need of company," she said with a smile that spoke to their hearts. "You grow more like your mother every day, Emily, and she was judged to be a great beauty in her time. Sit down. Ah, here is Lord Bridlington." She waved at Oliver, who came immediately at her signal.

"Lady Luxton, it is a pleasure to see you, as always. Miss Clifford. Miss Bracken," he said, bowing gracefully to them all. "My mother will be here in a while and I know she will be delighted to see you all again. You will allow me in the meantime to procure some refreshment for you?"

"Well, I for one am parched, and a drink would be most welcome," said Sophie.

He went to fulfil his assignment and Elizabeth said in a voice that could be heard only by Sophie and Emily, "You will have seen, I am sure, that several furtive glances have been thrown in our direction. Try if you can to behave as if there is nothing untoward. Rebecca Sedgewick is an old friend of mine, and it is to her credit that she has seen fit to invite you to her ball. We must now make what we can of this opportunity."

Sophie both delighted and saddened her by telling her of the decision not to purchase a new ball gown for fear of never having another opportunity to wear it and, with the addition of three further rows of bows and an overskirt of lustring in the same pale green, it was unrecognisable as the previous garment. Talk of fashion led them to relax into their normal manner. Oliver entreated Emily to dance and Sophie and Lady Luxton were joined upon her arrival by Lady Bridlington. There was no doubt as the evening progressed that Sophie was being ignored by a number of the assembled company. She had expected it. She had dreaded it. And the reality was worse than she had anticipated. Unable to control her trembling lip, she bit the inside in an attempt to hide her mortification.

Then something occurred to change everything. Lord Luxton arrived late in the company of Lady Jersey, whose carriage had pulled up behind his outside the house. He went directly to his mother and, still on his arm, Lady Jersey came with him. Not only that, but she remained with them for some twenty minutes, talking animatedly as was her fashion and engaging Sophie more than any other in conversation. It was enough. Lady Jersey was the arbiter of social behaviour. What was good enough for her, few would hesitate to emulate. Full of mischief, she delighted in her position of power. She would never have considered elevating one of whom she did not approve, but she had previously decided that fate had dealt Miss Clifford a difficult hand. The girl had breeding. Having done what she set out to do, she left them to bestow her favours upon others, but not before she had whispered into Sophie's ear, "Don't worry, my dear. You'll do now." And do she did. All at once her hand was being solicited for a dance.

Rufus escorted her into supper and confided, "Sally Fane was ever one to carry the crowd. I knew I might rely upon her to support you."

"You asked her?"

"Nothing so obvious. Let me only say that a small hint was sufficient to engage her interest. We go back a long way and I count her as a true friend."

"Once again you leave me in a position where I must express my thanks to you, Lord Luxton."

"Is it so hard, then, to do so?" he said with such a smile in his eyes that she could not help but respond.

"No, but I fear you must be growing bored with my continuing gratitude," she replied, her own smile reflecting his. "Until your arrival, and that of Lady Jersey, I felt destined to remain at your mother's side for the whole evening."

"Whereas now I doubt there is a dance remaining on your card." He became serious for a moment. "I think we may safely say that your position as an outcast is at an end. I thank God for it. You were made for better things than sitting meekly on the side."

She laughed aloud. "Oh no, Lord Luxton, not meekly, please." And with that the stern look left his face and the remainder of the evening was of unalloyed pleasure.

CHAPTER TWELVE

Sophie's salver no longer carried one lonely invitation but was in danger of spilling over onto the dresser upon which it stood. Days and evenings both were filled beyond capacity, and the only blot for Sophie was her father's continued insistence on remaining aloof from those places where members of the ton might remark and disapprove.

The days began to grow longer and Sophie, happier than she had ever been, found she had one new thing about which to be concerned. It had not escaped her notice that Oliver, always a frequent visitor, came more often to Hay Hill, nor that Emily was the reason he sought their company. She could not have been more delighted and smiled to think she was filling the role which had been designated for Miss Bracken. She would not leave them alone (doubtless Lord Luxton would have approved) but it was evident that it would not be long before Lord Bridlington declared himself and she had little hope of finding another whose company she so much enjoyed. She cast her mind about her acquaintance to see if there was someone who might fill the space she was so certain Emily would soon vacate. No-one came to mind and she put the problem aside, vowing to deal with it as necessity dictated. Necessity, however, had other things planned. One morning she received a note from Elizabeth Solgrave which sent her hurrying to Grosvenor Square.

"You will not believe how foolish I feel. I have been in that room a hundred times and I'm no stranger to the layout of the furniture. The footstool was where it has always stood, but that did not prevent me from falling over it and breaking my ankle.

Not only that but, as you can see, I hit my face as I went down and am displaying a most colourful eye through which I cannot, for the present, see anything at all."

"Oh, poor you. Is it very painful?"

"I fear my pride has suffered more than my physical wellbeing. But that brings me to the reason I asked you to come. Naturally I cannot go abroad looking like this and, in any case, it is nearly time to return to Ashby. With Lydia and Freddie still away, you would do me a great favour if you and Emily will come with me into Buckinghamshire. I realise what a huge sacrifice this will be to you, and Rufus strictly forbade me to ask you, but without being able to get around on my own and with my daughter away, well, I feel somewhat helpless."

Sophie could see how hard it was for Lady Luxton to ask for help. A proud woman, there was no doubt she would have preferred to manage on her own.

"You may tell Lord Luxton that I do not value his interference in this case. Ah, here he is now. I shall tell him myself. Good afternoon, sir. I would ask that in future you do not intervene on my behalf without consultation. How could you think I would hesitate to accompany your mama to Ashby when she has been so very kind to me?"

"I see you have a temper that matches your hair," he said with a smile that enraged her further. "Before you give added vent to your anger, I would like you to know that I did not wish to curtail your pleasure by dragging you back to the country."

"I would not consider it being dragged. How could you even think so or that something so frivolous would keep me from aiding a friend?" She turned to his mother and said, "If you would like me to accompany you in your travelling coach, I can leave tomorrow. It will not take long to put plans in place, and I know Emily will be delighted to visit Ashby. I will write to express my regrets to those of my acquaintance to whom I am promised, and we will be ready at your convenience." She did, however, wonder how delighted Miss Bracken would be to leave London and Lord Bridlington.

The freedom of being once more in the country was not lost upon Sophie. With her whole household moved to Ashby, and Oliver following them, life was not so very different from what it had been in London, aside from all the parties. She and Elizabeth both laughed at Bridlington when he presented himself. Neither was deceived when he said, "I was sure you ladies would be moped to death with so little to do, so I took it upon myself to join you. I'm certain Luxton will have no objection."

"My son is not with us, Lord Bridlington, but I'm sure you are right. He is at present visiting friends in the north, a commitment he made some time ago, I believe. His regret, having escorted us home, was that he was unable to remain more than a day or so. Your presence here will be a great advantage," she said with a mischievous smile. "You will be able to accompany Miss Clifford and Miss Bracken to parties for which we have already received one or two invitations, even in this short time. Under the circumstances, while I am unable to join them I would feel happier knowing you were in attendance upon them."

Oliver was acutely embarrassed. He had been certain he would find his friend at home and now felt he was imposing on Elizabeth's hospitality. She brushed his protestations aside.

"You must know you are welcome here at any time and, frankly, we are more than happy that you are here." The devilment in her made her add, "Of course, we would not wish to detain you, should you prefer to return to London."

Oliver had no desire to return to the capital. He welcomed the opportunity to spend more time with Emily and assured Lady Luxton that he would be only too delighted to escort the ladies wherever they might wish to go. A round of visits ensued which ensured that Sophie and Emily would not miss the delights of the city, but they also spent many happy hours, when Elizabeth chose to rest with her foot elevated, walking the grounds of Ashby or sitting quietly in the drawing room where Miss Bracken, who had a very melodious voice, would read aloud to them all. The weather, though there was still a chill in the air, proved kind and there were even days when it was warm enough for Elizabeth to sit on the terrace, albeit with a blanket over her knees, or to be wheeled around the flower garden in a wheelchair which had been acquired with the aid of Doctor Bolton. Sophie took every opportunity to promote the romance between Emily and Oliver. It seemed she had developed an interest in sketching and would sit with Lady Luxton while they strolled, within sight but effectively alone. In the privacy of Ashby, there was no need to maintain such vigilance as she had in town.

"Will they make a match of it, do you think?" Elizabeth asked her.

"I do hope so. They might have been made for each other."

"You are kind to sit with me and allow them such freedom. However, you will permit me to say that though your intentions are worthy, you have little talent for drawing."

"I know," Sophie said, laughing, "but it was all I could think of."

"Be serious for a moment, if you will. If, as I anticipate, there is to be a wedding, it will leave you once more in a difficult position. You have become like a daughter to me, and I would ask you to consider coming once more to live with me. No, don't cry," she added. "You must know how fond of you I have become."

Sophie stood and for a few moments paced up and down in an agitated fashion, before dropping to her knees beside Elizabeth and taking her hands. "If I cry, it is from happiness. I never had a mother, you see. To Lady Clifford I have only ever been her husband's daughter, and now it seems even that was a lie. In the short time I have known you, you have shown me more affection than anyone has in my whole life, and my gratitude for that knows no bounds."

"I am sensing a 'but'."

"Yes, though a regretful one. It would be so easy to give way to such temptation, but I have found also that I enjoy my independence. Having been confined for so long and with so many restrictions laid upon me, having my own establishment has given me, please don't laugh, a sense of pride in myself that I've never had before. I am not suggesting you would in any way impose restraints, but it would not be the same, you know."

She rose and resumed her pacing. Her heart was pounding, for she was quite overcome by the generosity of this woman who had, until a few short months ago, been merely a distant neighbour. Life at Ashby would never be dull. Her daily rides with Snowflake were always a joy and her hostess, when not confined by injury, was as sociable a person as one could hope to meet. Sophie would never be short of company or activity if she remained. But being her own mistress had opened her eyes to a side of herself she hadn't known before. Always having been subject to someone else's whim, she was now free to do as she pleased. It wasn't something she was ready to relinquish.

And then there was Joseph Templeton to consider. She did not feel she could invite him to Ashby, though she was as certain as she could be that neither Elizabeth nor her son would raise any objection. And there might be others in the future whom she would wish to welcome to her home. No, all things considered, it would be far preferable to live independently. Once more, she returned to Elizabeth's side and, because of the relationship they had established, she was able to explain exactly how she felt without giving offence.

"Then we must set ourselves to the task of finding you a home, for I think it will not be long before Emily leaves you," Elizabeth said as the couple approached.

Two days later, Oliver declared that trout was not the only thing he had caught that afternoon. He had returned from the stream to which Emily had accompanied him, promising to sit quietly by while he displayed his skill. Her feelings overcame her, though, when she saw the poor creature dangling on the end of a hook and she jumped to her feet and burst into tears. What could he do but try to console her?

"What a fool I am. I did not think. I should never have brought you with me. Such a villain, to cause you pain," he said, and he folded her into his arms. Naturally she laid her head on his shoulder. It was Emily who came first to her senses and stepped back. He released her immediately but only so that he could grasp her hands, imploring her forgiveness for his caddish behaviour.

"No, it is I who am to blame. Such foolishness. As if I didn't know what would happen. It's just that, when I saw…"

"Have I told you how adorable you are, Emily? Marry me and I will do all in my power to shield you from pain." The fish was forgotten and once more she was in his arms. Tilting her chin upwards, he placed his lips upon hers before raising his head to say, "You have made me the happiest man on earth," and smiling into her eyes. "Let us return to the house, for we have much to talk about. I must leave you for a few days to see your father. Naturally I need to ask his permission for us to wed."

Emily was rather of the opinion that her family would show as little interest in her marriage as they had in the rest of her life. She did somewhat naughtily contemplate their reaction when they learned she was to marry a lord, but would not confide in Oliver when he asked her what had made her laugh.

Their joy when they entered the drawing room was so tangible that the announcement came as no surprise to either of the ladies, who were just taking tea.

"Perhaps we might indulge in something a little stronger under the circumstances," Elizabeth said, and asked Bridlington to do the honours. "It is not every day we have a betrothal to celebrate."

"And I hope you will excuse my manners when I tell you that I shall be leaving tomorrow to seek permission from Emily's father to marry his daughter."

"I tried to tell him it wasn't necessary. That I am an independent woman and do not need his approval."

"To which I replied that I wanted to do everything in form. I will have no shadow of criticism falling upon my future wife." He was smiling still, but no one was in any doubt that he meant what he'd said. It was a very happy group who later sat down to supper.

"Though I fear I shall never again be able to eat trout," Emily remarked and was called upon to explain. Elizabeth's laughter was infectious, but she suggested that in future, when her affianced husband went hunting or fishing, she might perhaps remain at home and pursue more womanly occupations.

Sophie, so delighted for her friend, couldn't help but realise that her own situation had altered and she must contemplate rather sooner than she had anticipated what her next move might be. She fell asleep with the problem still on her mind. Oliver left straight after breakfast the next morning.

The day after that, Lord Luxton returned to Ashby. He had cut short his visit to the north on the pretext that he was concerned for his mother. The truth was, he had become so accustomed to seeing Sophie practically every day and it had come as a surprise to him how much he missed her.

He walked into the morning room, still in his riding clothes, and Sophie's breath caught in her throat as she saw how handsome he looked. He went first to Elizabeth, bestowing a token of affection upon her cheek before turning to Emily and then to Sophie. He bent over her hand, trying to conceal what he was sure would be plain to see in his deep chestnut brown eyes. He had spent years hiding behind a shelter of affability, so well-honed that he had come to believe it himself. But Miss Clifford had somehow penetrated his armour. The veil came down as he stepped away and he asked the ladies how they were enjoying themselves. Sophie, no less adept at masking her feelings, laughed and moved across the room to retrieve her sketchbook from where she had rested it against the back of a yellow damask-covered chair.

"You will see, sir, that I have been consigning various aspects of your beautiful grounds to paper. Sadly I am no expert, and each is virtually indistinguishable from the next. My talents, if I have any, must lie in another direction."

Rufus took the book and turned it this way and that, feigning an attempt to discern the difference between the top and the bottom before agreeing with her. "I am certain you have many talents, Miss Clifford, but sadly I must agree that sketching is not one of them."

"You are not a gentleman, sir. You might otherwise have pretended to admire them."

"But then I would have been caught out in a lie," he said, laughing. "Do you gain pleasure from the activity?"

"Strangely enough, as long as I have a companion with me, yes, I do. My hands cannot be still, you see. But the conversation is always more absorbing, so perhaps that is the reason they are so bad."

Emily came to stand beside Rufus, who was still contemplating the book in his hands. Leaning in, she added her own opinion that it might be for the best if none of the sketches were put on public view.

"Perish the thought. But I still enjoy the occupation and will continue with it, though I shall be careful not to display the products of my labour."

Lady Luxton demanded their attention from her chair and they all turned towards her. "Before you change your clothes for dinner, my son, I must tell you that we have some very exciting news. But it is not mine to tell. Emily?"

Emily blushed very prettily and informed him that Lord Bridlington had done her the honour of asking for her hand in marriage. "He has only yesterday left to speak with my father."

"Oliver has been here? I couldn't be more delighted, Emily. He is my best friend and you, cousin, have become very dear to me in these past few weeks. When are you to be married?"

Emily informed him that no arrangements had yet been put in place, as everything had happened so quickly. "But Lord

Bridlington did say he would send a notice to the *Morning Post* directly after speaking with my father."

"And is he returning to Ashby soon?"

"Yes, my lord, I believe we shall see him again within a very few days."

"The dog! I shall take great pleasure in congratulating him in person. If it is his intention to remain for a while, we may take the opportunity to bag a couple of rabbits, or maybe to fish in the trout stream."

He couldn't understand why all three ladies suddenly and seemingly spontaneously burst into laughter.

Rufus accompanied Sophie on her ride the next morning. There was no conversation as they cantered across country, but they paused by the stream to allow the horses to slake their thirst.

"Would you care to dismount and walk a while?" he asked her. "We can lead our mounts as we go."

She was only too ready to oblige and he lifted her down from the saddle, acutely aware of her proximity, but no more so than she. The ripples in the water twinkled as they caught the sunlight, and buds forming on the overhanging trees were a testament to the coming of spring.

For once oblivious to the beauty of his surroundings, Luxton stared fixedly ahead and said, "My mother has informed me that she asked you to remain at Ashby as her companion, but that you have declined." There was regret rather than reproach in his words.

Sophie threw him a quick glance, questioning, apologetic. "Yes, and I am aware of the debt I owe her. The debt I owe both of you, but you will understand my reasons, I am sure."

Still walking, still staring ahead, he said, "Of course. There is something else I would ask you to consider. I have watched you these last few months. You have had much to deal with, and I must say that you have behaved with dignity throughout. You have commanded my complete admiration, and I would beg that you do me the honour of becoming my wife."

Not the smoothest of proposals from a man renowned for his address, but his urbanity was overtaken by the onset of nerves. Sophie stopped in her tracks so suddenly that Snowflake walked into her and nearly knocked her over. Regaining her balance gave her time to consider how she might reply. A passing butterfly mirrored the fluttering of her heart. She had dignity, he thought, and he admired her. There was no mention of love.

Two thoughts were uppermost in her mind. The first was that she wanted nothing more than to spend the rest of her life with this man. The second was that he did not love her, for surely he would have said so if he did. Hard upon this thought was that there was no way she would marry anyone merely out of his respect for her, especially when she now realised what her own sentiments were. She wondered if it was the marriage of one of his closest friends and the betrothal of another that might have caused him to consider it was time he too took a bride. Taking a deep breath, she turned to face him.

"You do me a great honour, sir, but I believe that, should I ever wed, the relationship would have to be based on something more than admiration. I owe you so many debts, but I will not marry where there is no love."

Rufus thought he understood, believing she was saying that she did not love him. And so he didn't utter the words that rose to his lips and said instead that he hoped he might earn her affection in the future but would respect her decision. "I pray you will not allow this to bear upon our friendship, Miss Clifford, which I value most highly."

"As do I, and I hope most sincerely that we may carry on as before. Perhaps we should now return to the house, do you think?"

"Yes, of course. Allow me to help you mount."

He did so and they trotted back, each with their own thoughts and a sorrow that neither could express, and Sophie with a stronger than ever determination to find her own home, and quickly.

CHAPTER THIRTEEN

Somehow, both Sophie and Rufus were able to resume their former ease with each other, and Elizabeth had no apprehension of what had passed between them. She would have been sadly disappointed, as it had become her dearest wish to see her son united with her young friend. The likelihood seemed further away than ever when Sophie engaged an agent to find a suitable property for her. At least she was searching in the local area and it was to be hoped, therefore, that frequent contact would be maintained.

Oliver returned with the news that his prospective father-in-law had been willing to place the care of his daughter into his hands. Having first bolted to town to inform his mother in person of the forthcoming nuptials, he told them an announcement of the engagement would be posted the following day. Lydia and Freddie returned from their honeymoon to stay at Ashby for a few days before moving to Conroy's home in another county. He didn't maintain a house in London, choosing instead to put up at a hotel when he visited, and that was another thing he wanted to put in place for when he and his bride next visited the capital. Rufus was delighted for his sister and his friends but found himself wishing he could be sharing their joy on a more personal level. As for Sophie, she resigned herself to remaining single, for with her heart given away, she could not seek love elsewhere.

"My agent has sent me details of a house in Wigginton just south of Tring, and another nearby in Cholesbury, both of which look to be suitable. He is to take me there tomorrow," Sophie told Rufus when they were once again out riding, a habit they had not allowed to lapse despite their experience by the stream.

"Would you like me to accompany you? I have no other commitments."

"Is it not Lydia and Freddie's last day? You might prefer to remain here at Ashby."

"We will return in time to have supper with them in the evening. And we will be here to wave them off the next day."

"In that case, I would appreciate it very much. It may be that you will notice things I would not think of. I never paid too much attention at Charnwood, not being encouraged to 'interfere'."

"Then of course I will come. Is the agent coming to collect you?"

"No, I am to meet him there. All the more reason to be grateful for your escort," she said, green eyes smiling up at him. In truth, she would be glad of both his company and his advice. Independent as she was, this was a huge step for her and it was important to get it right.

The first house proved to be a huge disappointment, but Sophie fell in love with the property in Cholesbury on sight. It was designated a cottage, but with three storeys it was on a far larger scale than that term might imply. Climbing roses rambled around the front porch, too early in the season yet to be in flower but she could imagine how they might look in the summer. The house was set at the end of a drive which wound its way from the lane and a pond could be seen in the gardens to the left of the building. There was shrubbery on the other side and the whole effect was pleasing to the eye. The agent, a Mr Parish, had led the way from Wigginton to Cholesbury in his gig and welcomed Sophie and Rufus into the generously sized entrance hall.

"Do come in, Miss Clifford. Lord Luxton," he said and proceeded to show them around. A carved oak staircase ran from the centre of the hall, dividing to reach the first floor and extending upwards to a further level. On the first storey there were ample rooms in which to entertain as well as a smaller private sitting room. From the drawing room, large windows overlooked expansive grounds to the rear of the building.

"The drapes and furniture are all to remain if you wish," said Mr Parish. "I would suggest the burnished gold does much to enhance an already beautiful room, and the mouldings on the ceiling and walls give it a nice touch of character."

"Yes, a very comfortable room. I like it. Shall we move on now to the dining room?"

"Of course. If you would like to follow me, I shall take you there."

The dining room had the capacity to seat perhaps twenty people, which Sophie thought more than sufficient. Both she and Rufus approved each room in turn, going also to inspect the bedchambers before returning to the lower floor to see the kitchens and a library which was situated to the right of the entrance to the main hall. Neither found anything to displease them, and Sophie became increasingly excited as the tour progressed. Rufus, on the other hand, was a little subdued as he realised it would not be long before she moved from Ashby. However, he hid his feelings well and was able to utter the right amount of encouragement when she enthused in the carriage on the way home. There was an option either to rent the property or to purchase it outright, and Sophie professed a wish to do the latter.

"Rose Cottage will suit me admirably, and I see no reason not to make it my own. I believe I must tell Mr Parish that I wish to go ahead, do you not think so?"

"I noticed you spent considerable time examining the stable facilities," Rufus said, turning to smile at her with complete understanding. "They are well-equipped to accommodate Snowflake and any other horses and carriages you might require. I have to agree it is near perfect for what I understand to be your intentions."

"And it is convenient that I am in sympathy with the way it has been furnished. Having nothing of my own to bring, I will be left with nought to do but move in at my convenience."

"I must presume then that you will not remain long with us at Ashby."

She glanced at his profile as he concentrated on negotiating a particularly difficult stretch of the road and was fascinated to watch a muscle moving on the side of his face. "Do not think I am unconscious of how very accommodating you have been, but yes, I would like to move fairly soon. However, if you permit, I will remain until Lady Luxton's ankle is healed sufficiently for her not to require any aid. With Mr and Mrs Conroy about to leave, I would not wish to leave her unattended and, while I know you are devoted to her, there are some things that are best shared with another woman."

Could she but have known it, Rufus was delighted that she was to remain some little while longer, whatever the reason.

Oliver's stay was short-lived and, when he left, he took Emily with him. He was to escort her to London where his mama had invited her to stay until the wedding. Lady Bridlington had charged her son with telling Miss Bracken that she would be accompanying her on a round of various establishments, the purpose being to purchase bridal clothes. And she would not take no for an answer. Emily didn't bother putting up even a token resistance which she knew would be useless. It was fortunate that she had met the redoubtable old lady several times or she might otherwise have been in fear and trembling. As it was, she knew she could anticipate a shopping spree filled with pleasure.

After all the comings and goings, the next few days assumed a more peaceful pattern but the Solgraves and Sophie were all surprised one afternoon when they received a visitor in the person of Baron Clifford. Elizabeth was the first to recover.

"Forgive me if I do no rise, sir, but I have broken my ankle and must for the time being remain seated. Do please join us," she said, indicating a chair close to her own but some distance from Sophie's. Luxton acknowledged his bow and Sophie regained her wits, nodded at him and said she was delighted to see him. She was careful not to address him in any way, for she could no longer bring herself to call him Papa.

"Your mama and brother send their fondest wishes. A very pretty letter you wrote to me and, as you will not be returning to Charnwood, I have brought with me your mother's jewels."

Sophie was in no doubt that he referred to Harriet, for of a certainty her step-mama would not bestow anything upon her. While she had never regretted pressing her mother's locket upon Joseph Templeton, she had since become aware of how often she had fingered it when it was around her neck, either when she was agitated or in need of the comfort of knowing she retained a small part of her mother. She was surprised that Clifford had brought the jewels to her at all, for in her ignorance she would never have missed them. Perhaps she had misjudged him.

"It had been my intention," he continued, "to give them to you on the occasion of your betrothal to Francis. Sadly he tells me you have rejected his suit, a decision I hope you do not live to regret," he said, heavily stressing the last few words.

No, perhaps she had not misjudged him after all, and she most certainly resented him discussing her personal affairs in front of people who were, to him, relative strangers. Consequently, she thanked him politely but made no attempt to engage him in further conversation, to such a degree that, with no support from either Lady Luxton or her son, he judged it time to take his leave. The casket sat on a small table where Clifford had deposited it, and Sophie's eyes were drawn inexorably towards it.

"Why don't you take it to your room, my dear? Rufus and I perfectly understand if you wish to examine the contents in private. Also, as you have previously entrusted us with your confidence, I make no doubt that the sudden appearance of the baron has set you all on end and you may wish for some time to compose yourself."

Sophie thanked her for her compassion and lifted the box with trembling hands, the knowledge that Harriet must herself have touched it many times bringing a constriction to her throat.

Sophie placed her mother's casket on the dresser in her room and sat motionless for a while before reaching out to caress the tortoiseshell and bronze from which it was fashioned. Standing some two feet wide by one foot high, it was an imposing article which she judged to be French. With a pounding heart, she lifted the clip and raised the lid. There were various compartments containing more jewels than she had ever before seen assembled together. She picked a sapphire necklace and held it up to examine it. She admired its simplicity, though it was evidently an expensive piece. It did not best suit her colouring, but she could imagine how it might have enhanced her mother's blond hair and blue eyes. She wished she might have a likeness of her mama and realised that in her whole life she'd had no contact with Harriet's family. It came as a shock, and she wondered why it had never before occurred to her. Even though their daughter had died in childbirth, surely her grandparents would have wanted to meet her. Had it not been for Joseph Templeton, she would not even have known their name. Munro, he had said. She had never heard the family mentioned, so it was doubtful they were local to Charnwood. She wondered where they might reside and why they had never contacted her. If their aim had indeed been to marry their daughter into the gentry, would they not have striven to maintain the connection? She had so many questions. It was to her father she would look for answers. He had written to tell her he was returning to his family home which was situated in Yorkshire and she knew, more from what he didn't say than the information he imparted, that it would be quite an ordeal for him after so long abroad. His hope was to visit her once she had established herself. Had he not told her that in their youth he and Harriet had been neighbours? It was to the north then that she would look to find her roots.

Absentmindedly she returned the necklace to its place and retrieved an emerald ring. She placed it on the smallest finger of her left hand and held it up to see the effect. It caught the light as she turned her hand this way and that. She closed the casket lid and sat back to reflect. *I will look no more until I am settled in my own home. Then I will examine my mother's jewels at my leisure.* But she twiddled the ring which remained on her hand, and uppermost was the question of how she would trace a family whose existence she had never even thought to question.

Sophie remained two weeks longer at Ashby. It was both a pleasure and a pain. Lord Luxton had put all his plans on hold until his mother was once more able to get around as before. At least, that was the reason he gave. He accompanied Sophie twice more to Cholesbury where minor changes were taking place at Rose Cottage. His tiger, Wilfred, perched on the back of his carriage could not help but wonder if the master had at last met his fate. But surely by now, had it been the case, the whole household would have known. He wasn't in Bixby's confidence. That superior valet would have deemed it beneath his touch to gossip with one so below his own station. But Wilfred thought he sniffed something in the air. He'd have been pleased, too, for any woman who was such a clipping rider as Miss Clifford commanded his respect. However, when Sophie left Buckinghamshire, so too did Lord Luxton and Lady Luxton, all three to different destinations. If the tiger thought his master like a bear with a sore head, he refrained from voicing the observation.

The countess went to pay a visit to her daughter which was to last for several weeks. The earl returned to the capital in an attempt to lose himself in gentlemanly pursuits and Miss Clifford removed to Cholesbury with only her abigail to lend her countenance and, though a hired companion was to join her shortly, she had no expectation of finding another Emily. Her reasons were not to protect her own reputation by observing convention but to prevent anything further sullying her father's name. Though she had every intention of becoming acquainted with her new neighbours, for she was not by nature reclusive, Sophie knew that much of her time would be focussed on finding her long lost family, something that was fast becoming an obsession with her. To this end, she invited Joseph Templeton to visit as soon as was convenient for him.

CHAPTER FOURTEEN

Sophie had been living in her new home for barely a month when her father arrived. Not until she saw him did she realise how much she had missed his company. His own joy was plain to see, and he hugged her as if trying to make up for the lost years. Responding to his embrace she said, "It makes me wish I had chosen to reside in Yorkshire. We might then have seen more of each other than is practical at present."

"Not so, for it is doubtful I shall be spending much time there myself. While I have a certain responsibility to maintain my family home near Sowerby, I long ago lost any emotional connection with it. The years of travelling have become, for me, a way of life, and were it not for you I should have been off long before now. Perhaps I was born to be a vagabond."

Her stricken look was evidence of how little this appealed and, though she would not have dreamed of coercing him, she couldn't help but ask, "You would leave? When we have only just found each other?"

"You will not be rid of me so easily, my darling girl. My journeying will be curtailed and I shall come to see you often, but my feet will not be still for long." He smiled ruefully as he accepted the cup of tea she handed to him. "I cannot be in Yorkshire without being reminded every moment of Harriet. The years between have served to ease the pain a little, but there is not a day I do not think of her. Going home, seeing those places where we were together, is like the eruption of an old wound."

Sophie didn't answer. Though her father looked at her, he was plainly seeing some long ago vision and she would not intrude. After several moments he seemed to give himself a mental shake and smiled upon her once more. "The house goes to a distant cousin when I die. I make no doubt he has been hoping these many years to hear of my demise. It's a pretty place but, as I have tried to explain, the memories it holds for me are not at all pretty."

"Do my grandparents still live?" she asked, with no little trepidation. "You told me that you and my mother lived in close proximity and that, forgive me, she was forced into marriage with Clifford for the sake of a title. They were never mentioned at Charnwood and somehow, I don't know how, it never occurred to me to ask about my other family. Only recently have I wondered why they never came to visit."

"Yes, they are there still. My understanding is that they live quietly now. In spite of all their riches, they have been unable to buy happiness. I have not seen them, of course. This is merely hearsay. Are you saying you would like to meet them?"

Did she want to meet them? It seemed unlikely they desired to have anything to do with her. Surely, otherwise, they would have contacted her during these twenty-one years. But as surely as she had inherited her father's hair, Munro blood ran through her veins. They might reject her out of hand, but she had to know.

"Can you arrange it?"

"Personally? I doubt it."

Disappointment was writ over her face.

"They will not wish to hear from me, I am sure. But I can give you their direction. There is no reason why you cannot write to them yourself if you choose to do so. In fact, I would recommend you take that course of action. Better they refuse you in a letter than close the door in your face."

Sophie raised her hand to brush away a wisp of hair that had escaped and fallen over her eyes and, as she did so, Joseph smiled, a smile she had not seen before.

"What is it, Papa?"

"You are wearing your mother's ring. It was my mother's too. I gave it to Harriet when I asked her to be my wife. No-one knew of our secret betrothal and she tried to return it to me when she discovered that fate was to turn her life in another direction. I refused. I wanted so badly for her to have something to remember me by. I wonder if she ever wore it."

· Sophie explained how she had come by the emerald, and the other jewellery as well. She offered to fetch the casket and show him the contents but Joseph refused.

"I think not, my dear. Most would have come from her own family. I doubt Clifford would have bestowed much of value upon her, and if he did I don't wish to see it. You have Harriet's ring and, thanks to your generosity, I have her locket. It is enough."

Joseph remained in Cholesbury for another two weeks, during which time he and Sophie spent many hours walking, riding or just seated in conversation. She learned about his travels abroad and how it was a life that had suited him well. He was promised to friends in Scotland but would return before leaving the country again or, at the very least, would apprise her of his movements. Meanwhile, two things had happened. Sophie's new companion, Caroline Ward, arrived at Rose Cottage, a spinster in her early thirties who, though she lacked Emily's vivacity, shared with Sophie a love of horses. It would be common ground enough for them. Secondly, a letter had been sent to Mr and Mrs Munro. At the time of Joseph's departure, no reply had been received.

"I should have heard by now," Sophie whispered to him plaintively on his last evening.

"It is possible they are away from home, or that your letter was delayed. Or even that they have yet to reply. But you must also prepare yourself for the possibility that you will not hear from them, Sophie. If that should be the case, you must put this search behind you."

She raised her face to him, her eyes full of sadness and longing. "I know, but I have built up my hopes over these past few weeks and it would be such a let-down if it all came to nothing."

"You are a young woman of great courage, Sophie. If that happens, I am confident you will find a way to bear it. Now, let me tell you about the time I visited Florence. A wonderful city. Maybe I can take you there one day."

Sophie waved goodbye to her father the next morning and took Snowflake out in an attempt to dispel her sorrow. A letter was waiting for her when she returned.

My dear Sophie,

My wife and I were delighted to receive your letter, which came as something of a shock to us both. You will forgive me, I am sure, if I couch my enthusiasm with a modicum of caution. Our daughter's death so long ago struck us both down with a blow from which we have never recovered. She was our only child. You have questioned why we had no contact with you and this is something we are happy to make clear — if you prove to be who you say you are.

I do not know what your father told you, but I am a self-made man and proud of it. You will find no gentry on this side of the family but what you will discover, and I make no bones about it, is huge wealth, honestly earned. If I tell you that over the years many charlatans have approached me, purporting to have just such a connection as you claim, you will understand why I have reservations as to your identity. All have been fortune-hunters, and I sent each of them packing with a flea in the ear.

Nothing would give us greater joy than for you to authenticate your status. If you are a fraud, you will be uncovered. If you are genuinely our granddaughter and can demonstrate this, you will make two old people very happy and we will welcome you with open arms.

Yours in hope
James Munro

Sophie was standing in the hall as she read the letter, having paused only to remove her riding gloves and lay down her crop. She realised that she was shaking and sat down on a small chair which stood against the wall adjacent to the library.

"Are you all right, miss?" the footman asked. He was a young man who had been engaged by Mr Parish and this was his first position. He could see that the colour had drained from Miss Clifford's face and, while he didn't think it was his place to put himself forward, he judged it wise in the circumstances. "Would you like me to fetch Miss Ward?"

Sophie looked up, the letter still clutched in her hand, then her expression cleared. "Thank you, Arthur, I will be recovered in a few moments. I do not hide that I have received some disturbing news, but I shall be well shortly. Perhaps you could order some tea to be brought to me in the library. I should like to be alone for a while."

"Yes, miss. Of course."

"Thank you, Arthur. I appreciate your concern."

When she felt able to stand without fear of falling over, Sophie rose and entered the room next to her. She sat at a small table, trying to digest what she had just read and, when Arthur brought in the tea, she acquiesced when asked if she would like him to pour it for her. It wasn't his duty to do so, and he hoped he hadn't crossed the line. "You said you wanted to be alone, miss, so I thought it best to bring it myself. I'll be just outside the door if you need me."

The tea was soothing and the letter, having been read three times, was laid upon the table. Sophie leaned on her elbow and looked out of the window to where blossom adorned the trees, spring now being well-established. She had no written proof of her identity, but what she did have was Joseph Templeton's hair and her mother's casket. The first would make her instantly recognisable as his daughter, but did they know that Harriet had borne his child? If not, the knowledge was likely to engender even more grief, and it was this that caused her to hesitate. But she had come this far. She couldn't back away now. Moving from the table to the desk, she wrote a reply indicating that she would, if convenient, visit them following a pre-arranged trip to London.

CHAPTER FIFTEEN

Had it been any other engagement Sophie would have sent her apologies and journeyed straight into Yorkshire, but an invitation had been received to attend the wedding of Miss Emily Bracken to Lord Oliver Bridlington and it was to take place the following week at St George's in Hanover Square. She was to stay once more in Grosvenor Square with Elizabeth Solgrave, who had returned to town after visiting her daughter, and, while every instinct was urging her to head in an entirely different direction, she would not for the world have given offence to any of the interested parties. And so it was that, with her thoughts elsewhere, Sophie set out for London on a beautifully sunny day to attend the nuptials of two very close friends.

It had not escaped her that she would once again be thrown into close company with Lord Luxton. It was a prospect she regarded with mixed feelings. She could not deny that she missed his society. Never in her life had she felt so comfortable in a man's company, or so disconcerted. He had the ability to make her feel valued as she had never valued herself. Had he not said he admired her? But admiration was not enough, and she hoped sincerely that he would not renew his proposal. She wanted also to discuss with him her forthcoming visit to Halifax. Rufus would be able to temper both her enthusiasm and her trepidation, she was sure. She found the opportunity to discuss this with him the day before the wedding. Caroline was in the drawing room with Elizabeth when Sophie entered the hall just as Rufus was coming out of his library.

"I wonder if you might spare me a few moments, my lord. There is a subject on which I would like to seek your advice."

"Of course. Would now be convenient? We shall not be disturbed in here," he said, moving back so she might enter the room ahead of him. He went to stand by the huge marble fireplace, one gleaming hessian resting on the hearth. He was able from this position to see that she was much agitated, twisting a kerchief between her fingers. "You seem to be distressed. Would you like me to leave you here alone for a while so that you may recover?"

Her glance flashed to his face, grateful for his speedy understanding, but she declined and smiled somewhat ruefully. "What, ban you from your own sanctum? Of course not, and you are right in your observation. You know so much of my circumstances that I have no hesitation in speaking to you now. I do not ask for advice. At least, I don't think so. But I have something on my mind which will gain clarity, I am sure, if I can but speak my thoughts aloud."

"Then I am at your disposal. I have no pressing engagements, and Miss Ward is very able to entertain my mother. It seems they have taken to each other rather well. You are lucky in your choice of companions, Miss Clifford. Take your time."

She took a deep breath. "I have written to my grandparents and received a reply a few days before I came to London. Perhaps it would be best if you read what my grandfather has said. It will give you a better understanding of the situation." She withdrew James Munro's letter from the reticule on her arm and handed it to him.

He took it and returned to the fireplace to read. "Have you such proof?" he asked, coming directly to the point.

"I have my mother's jewellery box. I am as certain as I may be that most of its contents were in her possession before she married Clifford. We are satisfied, are we not, that he had designs on her fortune, and this does not lead me to believe he was a man deeply in love who would have bestowed valuable gifts upon his wife. As such, they will surely recognise the pieces, even at this distance in time. The casket itself is not engraved, but I would suspect that too came from them."

"I think you are right. Would this not then be sufficient justification of your claim?"

Sophie paused before voicing her next fear. "It is possible that it came to me by foul means, is it not? If I were indeed an imposter, who knows to what lengths I might have gone? There has been no contact for so many years, I must assume they would not know my true circumstances."

She could see understanding writ upon his face. "Yes, I see. And how to refute that?"

"There is a way and it is for that very reason I seek your advice, or at least your ear. You have met my father. I think there can be no doubt as to our relationship, and he has himself told me his story. But Joseph Templeton's suit was rejected by the Munros. My grandfather has said there is something he is happy to clarify, look, here," she said, pointing to the relevant part of the letter, which he had returned to her. "But what might it be? Are they aware of the continuing relationship between him and my mother after her marriage? It might break their hearts to learn she had cuckolded her husband. They were ruthless enough to sacrifice their only daughter in the pursuit of their ambition. But the ambition was for her, not for themselves. To find it was all for nothing, what might that do to them? I have been turning it around and around in my head ever since I received this letter. There are so many possibilities. They might hate me, for was I not in effect the cause of my mother's death? They might hate themselves. They certainly will have no fondness for Joseph. You can see, can you not, why I needed to have someone to talk to? However, I fear it has been to no avail. The way forward is no clearer than it was half an hour ago."

"Don't be so hasty, Sophie." She chose to ignore his use of her given name. "I can see exactly the problems you outline. You said you wanted me to listen. Would you also like my opinion?"

"Very much so, whether I like it or not. It will be good to have another's point of view."

He sat in a chair close to hers and smiled reassuringly. Already she felt better.

"Let us consider for a moment," he said. "There are risks, I see that. But you are a woman who is prepared to face obstacles. It is, as I have said before, one of the things I most admire in you." That word again! "What if you choose not to go? You must wonder for the rest of your life what might have been. And what of your grandparents? One cannot admire what they did in the past, but it isn't unusual for such arrangements to be made. They have implied that it would give them great joy to be able to acknowledge you. Can you deny them that opportunity? You have opened Pandora's box. The evils have already spilled out. What is left to you but to follow the hope?"

It was only a few short weeks since Sophie had stood in this same church watching the joining together of Lydia and Freddie Conroy and, as Emily and Oliver exchanged vows, she thought how grateful she was for the accident that had brought these people into her life. No doubt there would always be a part of herself that she would keep private. It was a habit she had learned at Charnwood and one that would be hard to break. She would never know how she had put up with the oppression for so long, but she had broken free, and only at the expense of suffering a headache and the loss of her dignity. She owed that oak tree gratitude and resentment in equal measure. From a pew on the other side of the aisle, Rufus saw the smile playing around her mouth and wondered what she was thinking.

With the wedding over, Sophie turned her attention to the details of her journey north. It would take some days to travel to Halifax. Having brought most of what she required with her to London, she decided not to divert to Cholesbury but instead to have any other necessary items conveyed from her home to the nearest coaching inn on the Great North Road and held in readiness for her arrival.

"I was undecided as to what I might need in London, so I carried my mother's casket with me. In any case, I like to have it by me. It has become a most cherished possession. I was a little nervous of highwaymen, I must confess," she told Luxton. "As a precaution, I have decided to hire a guard as well as a coachman to conduct me to my grandparents' home."

"I beg you will allow me to escort you. I have a property in Yorkshire which my agent has been encouraging me to visit for longer than I care to say. It would be a good opportunity to fulfil the obligation and, in addition, it would give me great pleasure to tell him that I have, after all this time, complied with his wishes. He is a good man but a little over-zealous on occasion."

He did not miss the fleeting expression of indecision on her face before she replied, "I should be grateful indeed. Not only for the added security but also for the company. Caroline is sadly subject to being indisposed on long journeys and is likely to retire early each time we stop."

He chose not to question her hesitation. "Do you have time to remain in London while I send word to Edward Boyle? He is at present at Ashby and it may be that he has some tasks he wishes to charge me with. Also," he said with a grin, "he will be able to remind me of my people's names. I admit I am hopeless, particularly when it is so long since I was last there, but my agent knows every man and woman who has ever worked for me. It would not do for me to give anyone the cut, especially not those who are in my service."

Sophie laughed but admired the solicitude he employed in making his dependents feel they were valued. Growing serious again, she said, "Yes, of course I will wait. It is not only for your company that I am grateful. I am apprehensive as to what my reception will be when I reach my destination. Should the worst happen, your support will, I know, be invaluable to me."

She could not know how close Rufus was to declaring his love for her. All he wanted to do was take care of her, but he had the sense to realise, should she refuse him, how uncomfortable it would be to make such a journey in Sophie's company with so much hanging between them. Besides, there was no reason to suppose she had changed her mind since his last fumbled attempt. What she most needed now was someone she could rely on, who would not add to the considerable anxiety she was already experiencing. He kept his own counsel.

Because of the effect that travelling in a coach had on Caroline, the journey took even longer than anticipated.

"Had I been permitted to ride instead, I could have carried on from dawn to dusk. I have never understood why I am always so afflicted in this way. I am so very sorry to be holding you up, Sophie."

With the colour drained from her face and a tightening about her mouth, it was quite evident that she was suffering greatly, and Sophie could feel only sympathy for her plight. "What fun that would have been. I also feel the restrictions of being enclosed in a carriage for the best part of a day. But the weather is fine, and it is early enough in the afternoon for us to sit quietly in the inn's garden a while so you may recover your composure. Unless you would prefer the peace of your bedchamber?"

"No, this lovely sunshine is just what I need. Have you seen there is a stream running at the bottom of this slope? A lovely place to relax for an hour or so."

"I agree. Perhaps Lord Luxton would prefer to stretch his legs and join us later," Sophie said, looking up at him and sending a silent message.

Taking the hint, Rufus went for a stroll, happy in the knowledge that after an early supper he would have her to himself after Caroline retired. This became the pattern for each day and, as their journey progressed, their love deepened. He talked often of his travels abroad and brought to life places she had never seen. She spoke of her life at Charnwood, where the only times she had really been carefree was when riding Snowflake and, before her, a beloved pony she had named Chatterbox.

"Chatterbox?"

"She made little noises all the time. When we were riding. In her stall. Even when I was grooming her, something I insisted on doing myself. I always felt she was trying to have a conversation with me. When I grew too large for her to carry me, I begged to be allowed to keep her. For once Clifford permitted me to have my way. She only passed away a year ago and I miss her still."

Their silences were as comfortable as their conversations, and it was a time of contentment for them both but, as they approached Halifax, Sophie became apprehensive and there was little he could do to allay her fears.

CHAPTER SIXTEEN

They arrived at Munro Manor in the middle of a fine afternoon. It was an imposing building, larger even than Ashby, built in the Palladian style and designed to impress. James Munro was more than happy to display the product of his endeavours, but all was done with surprising subtlety and the effect was pleasing. As Rufus handed her down from the carriage, Sophie could see her grandparents standing on the steps, waiting to greet them. Her grandfather was huge and she would have taken him for a much younger man, had she not known better. Nancy Munro was diminutive but no less sprightly than her husband.

"Come along then, come along. Let's have a good look at you," Munro said, his voice thick with a Yorkshire accent. Sophie could sense that he was anxious and this helped relax her own nerves.

"I am so happy to be here, sir. You cannot know. But allow me to introduce to you Lord Luxton, who has been kind enough to escort me here. And Miss Caroline Ward, my companion."

"Yes, yes, come in. We will do the pretty when we are inside." He led the way through a large entrance hall to a relatively small room which was furnished with impeccable and very expensive taste. "This is where we sit, Nancy and me, when we want to be cosy. There's a much grander room along the corridor," he said, waving his hand in no particular direction, "but we're more comfortable in here. We don't much like doing the formal. So, take off your pelisse and bonnet and make yourself at home."

Nancy Munro gasped as Sophie removed the pretty confection to reveal her hair in all its glorious colour. Her spouse too was for once silent.

"You are shocked, as I feared you would be."

James seemed visibly to pull himself together. "You, Luxton, are you in Miss Clifford's confidence?"

"I am, sir, but if you prefer me to leave the room I will do so."

"And I prefer you to remain," Sophie said quickly, "though perhaps Miss Ward might be escorted to her chamber. This is no affair of hers and, in any case, she does not travel well and would, I believe, be grateful for some respite."

The old man smiled. "I see you are in the habit of organising things to your own wishes. Well, I'm the same road, so you'll get no objection from me." He rang the bell and asked the footman to show Caroline to her bedchamber. "And is this affair any concern of yours?" he continued, turning to Rufus.

"Only in as much as Miss Clifford has asked me to support her. I will try not to allow my presence to be an impediment to you reaching an understanding."

"Very well, you may stay." Turning to Sophie, James said, "You will see that Mrs Munro and I are in no doubt as to who your real father is. There can be no mistake. Forgive me, but you will recall that when I wrote to you I demanded proof that you are indeed my Harriet's daughter. This is not proof. It shows only that you were sired by Templeton. It is not enough."

Sophie realised this was as hard for him as for her. She suspected he would like nothing more than for her to show him and his wife something that would leave them in no doubt as to her true identity. Would the casket be enough? "There is something in my luggage that I would show you. If you will excuse me, I will retrieve it from where it was left in the hall."

She rose, but Luxton was before her. "Allow me, Miss Clifford. I will bring it to you."

The three sat in silence for the few moments it took him to return. He placed the jewellery box on a small table and removed the cloth that had been covering it. James and Nancy both gasped audibly. Nancy was, if anything, paler than before. James was quiet for a few moments and, taking a kerchief from his pocket, wiped his brow.

"I gave this casket to my Harriet on her sixteenth birthday. Do you mind?" he asked, indicating that he would like to open it.

"Of course not."

He picked up a necklace and a brooch, and then went through the rest. "I remember every single piece and the occasions upon which they were given. But there is one thing missing. A pearl necklace that her mother bestowed upon her on her marriage to Clifford. Where is it?"

"I have never seen such a thing. This only came into my possession very recently, when the baron gave it to me after I had left Charnwood. I was unaware before of its existence."

He uttered one word. "Shameful!"

"Perhaps, but I hope it is sufficient evidence that I am who I say."

"How am I to know that it isn't stolen?"

Rufus moved to stand behind Sophie and placed his hand on her shoulder, gripping a little to give her comfort. She sighed, a pitiful sound that was more like a rasp. "You are not to know, and I have no more. Nothing further to authenticate my claim."

"You are wrong," said the little woman who had neither spoken nor moved, except to clutch at her throat, since they'd entered the room. "If you are indeed my granddaughter, I can show you irrefutable proof." She stood up and moved towards Sophie. Rufus stepped back a pace. "Do me the favour of turning back the cuff of your left sleeve, my child."

Sophie had no idea what was to come next but complied immediately with the request.

"Now turn your arm over so that your palm faces upwards and push the sleeve away." With shaking hands, Nancy took the proffered arm and raised it slightly, peering at a spot between wrist and elbow. "It is here! James, it is here! She is indeed our granddaughter," she said, before fainting clean away on the floor.

Rufus swept her up and laid her on a chaise longue while Sophie ran into the hall to ask for some smelling salts. A while later Nancy was recovered enough to listen as James explained.

"We saw you only once when you were a babe. After that we were forbidden access. There was barely a hair on your head, so we had no indication of what was to come. What we did see was a birthmark in the shape of a strawberry. I have never forgotten how Nancy caressed it as she cradled you in her arms, the only time she has ever been able to do so. So now you understand how we were so able to eliminate the imposters who came before you."

"I never even thought about the mark. It is so much a part of me that it didn't ever assume any distinction. But why did you never come to see me, or write to me even?" Sophie asked, sitting on the floor beside her grandmother and holding her hand.

"Not many days after we returned to Halifax, I received a letter from your father, as I thought he was, telling me and my

Nancy that we were never again to set foot in Charnwood nor to try to contact you in any way. He said that he was in possession of some information that would blacken our daughter's name forever and that he would reveal it if we tried to do so. We had no idea what it might be, but we had found out since the marriage how terribly mistaken we had been in Clifford. Where before he had been charming, now he looked down upon us. All pretence was at an end, for he had achieved his aim. No fancy title is enough to compensate for the sacrifice we forced Harriet to make. We know that now." He paused as his voice broke and then continued on. "All these years he has been happy enough to take the money we sent for you, Sophie, with never a word as to how you were doing. Well, we will take our guilt to our graves and deservedly so, but we had long ago given up any hope of seeing you. Who knew what poison that man might have told you about us?"

"You were never mentioned. I didn't even know that I had grandparents, for I never questioned it."

"We have much more to discuss, but perhaps now would be a good time for you to go to your rooms and get ready for dinner. All this talk has given me a healthy appetite. Luxton, I thank you for your care of our child. It has been an ordeal for us all, but hopefully we can now look forward to a happier future."

Nothing further was discussed as they dined because Caroline had joined them, and no-one felt it appropriate to speak in front of her. Rufus asked if he might leave the ladies at the manor while he journeyed to his own estates some fourteen or fifteen miles away near Leeds.

"I shouldn't be gone more than three days, four at most."

"Then I hope you will be able to extend your stay when you return. Now that we have found her, we are not yet ready to relinquish our granddaughter. You are welcome to remain here for as long as suits you, and reet glad we'll be if you can."

"You are very kind. I shall remain at Miss Clifford's disposal."

"Very well then. So, you have property nearby. Not your main one, I'll be bound."

Rufus found himself warming to this man. He was straightforward and, when he asked questions, it was not because he was unduly prying but instead was so evidently displaying an interest.

"You're right. My family home is in Buckinghamshire, but there are three others in different parts of the country. I'm ashamed to say I do not get to visit them as often as I should. I am hoping this will be an opportunity to engage with my tenants."

"Farmers, are they?"

"Mostly, yes. Sheep farming, a subject I know very little about."

"Well, I can say without puffing up my own consequence that it's something I know a great deal about. I made my money running a mill. You'd be amazed how many different grades of wool there are. I could bore you for hours. Probably will when you come back." They were standing on the terrace blowing a cloud, having left the ladies inside. There was a full moon and Rufus was conscious of receiving a hard stare from the other man. "Got an eye on our girl, have you?" he asked, coming to the point abruptly as Rufus assumed he always would.

"Is it so obvious? She won't have me, sir. I'm afraid I made a mull of it."

James rubbed his chin with his thumb. "I'm thought to be a fair judge of people and I can tell you this, young man." Rufus felt he was back in university and being addressed by one of his lecturers. "If I'd recognised in Harriet and Templeton what I see now in you and our Sophie, we wouldn't be in the pickle we are today. Blow me if I ever saw two people more in love. If you want my advice, which you probably don't, you youngsters never do, you won't take no for an answer next time. That's all I have to say on the subject. Time to join the ladies, I think."

Rufus had no opportunity to be alone with Sophie before he left for Leeds the next morning and consequently didn't put Munro's suggestion to the test. Borrowing a horse — his host would not consider him hiring one — he rode away whistling, much as he had on the day he'd first encountered her lying by the road. Her grandfather was a shrewd man, there could be no doubting that. And he had himself seen glimpses in the last week that had given him cause to hope. Armed with the information he'd received from Edward Boyle, he spent the next few days diligently carrying out his long overdue duties. None to whom he spoke with his natural charm could have imagined how eager he was to be on his way back to Halifax.

CHAPTER SEVENTEEN

Rufus had much time to consider Sophie's situation during his ride back from Leeds and it was something he wanted to discuss with her, sooner rather than later. Even in the short time he'd been at Munro Manor, a lot of information had come to light. It was evident that her parents had settled a considerable sum on Harriet upon her marriage. It was obvious too that Sophie had been provided for throughout her childhood and that some arrangement had been made that had left her a wealthy woman. What hadn't been in evidence before was that she was her grandparents' sole heir, and her fortune would increase upon their demise by an amount at which Luxton could only hazard a guess. Certainly Sophie herself had never considered such a situation. Just as certainly, Clifford and his stepson had. It became clearer now why they were so keen on a marriage between her and Francis Follet. Lucky for her indeed the day she'd had her accident.

His conclusions left him with another dilemma. The encouragement he had received from James Munro had hugely lifted him and it had been his intention to press his suit as soon as possible upon his return. Armed now with the information he had and the inference it contained, he would feel less than happy to propose marriage when her financial status was almost certainly superior to his own, if not now then in prospect. He was a very wealthy man in his own right but was left with little doubt as to the riches his host had amassed. When he stopped to consider it, he'd always known it was his duty to marry and produce an heir, but this was no longer his main reason for wishing to wed. However, a match with his chosen bride now seemed to present a very unequal union. While he was more than eager to see Sophie again, he was no longer whistling.

The change in atmosphere when Luxton returned to Munro Manor was discernible. He and Sophie were standing on the terrace that first evening, waiting for the rest to join them for dinner, and it was their first opportunity for some private conversation. Her grandparents had welcomed her with open arms, she said, and Nancy Munro, though tiny as ever, seemed to have grown in stature. During his four-day absence, their granddaughter had been subject to an extensive tour of the house, had been introduced to various aspects of James's business — he not being of the opinion that these things should be only in the masculine domain — and, most enjoyable of all, had ridden all over the estate.

"Grandpapa no longer rides, but he provided me and Caroline with an escort and we have galloped all over the place. The country around here is breathtaking. You may imagine how delighted she was to be partaking of her favourite pastime. You would not have recognised her from the poor girl who accompanied us into Yorkshire."

"I see you have had a splendid time. I too have been initiated into the world of sheep farming and will perhaps have a greater understanding when Edward Boyle wishes to discuss some aspect with me. Have you been to your grandfather's mill yet?"

"No, for it is something he is particularly keen for you to see as well. In any case, I do not think we could have crammed it in, so busy have we been."

Rufus spoke spontaneously, words he had told himself he wouldn't say. "You had no time then to notice my absence?" He could have kicked himself. Even to his own ears he sounded clumsy. Sophie looked at him quizzically, her head on one side, and he longed to take her into his arms.

"How can you think so when we have shared so much? Everything I saw I wanted you to see too. Also, Grandpapa credited me with more comprehension than I had. He was bombarding me with so many details, I would have appreciated an enlightenment which I'm certain you would have been able to give me." She smiled broadly at him, trusting that he would enjoy the humour as much as she, but he remained serious, and still he held his own counsel. He changed the subject.

"Your grandmother seems to be a changed woman from the one who greeted us on the steps just a few days ago."

"Indeed she is. And did I tell you, she said she would have known me without any proof. That although our colouring is quite different there is a look about me of Harriet that she could not mistake. I suspect she had lost all hope of any contact. The baron did his work well. It is my belief that she has spent the last twenty-one years in mourning. I can never take my mother's place in her heart and I am certain she will never be able to rid herself of the guilt she has carried for so long, but there is a new hope which shines from her eyes and is apparent in the way she holds herself. This is no frail elderly lady but a woman who has found a new reason for living. You cannot know how much it means that I am the cause for this change. Nor how grateful I am that you came with me on this journey."

Still he didn't declare himself. Could anything have been more evident than the invitation she was offering him? He did not take it up and she turned away, disappointed that she had misread his feelings over these past several days.

"I don't come here much these days," James Munro told Sophie and Rufus as he drove them to the mill the following day, insisting on taking the reins himself, "but I like to poke my nose in every now and then, just so my people know I'm still alive. It's a bit different from when I started. I began with a smallholding and built myself up over the years. And this is what I ended up with," he said with pride, as they turned a bend in the road and an enormous building came into view.

It was impressive by any standards, something they both acknowledged. Rufus had seen many such constructions in recent days but none had been larger than this one. As they got down from the carriage, he and Sophie could see the huge wheel on the waterside. The river was wide here and flowing swiftly, and Rufus remarked that Munro has chosen his spot well.

"Happen I'll tell you summat about the industry if you'd like to know more. But come inside and you'll see for yourselves."

Nothing could have been more apparent than the respect and affection in which James Munro was held as they toured the mill, and as he engaged with the workers it was easy to understand why. He might have declared that he didn't visit frequently, but he knew every man's name and took the time to ask after their wives and children. "And Flitwick tells me your son will be coming to work here soon," he said to one. "I'll be sure to come and have a word with him. Tell him what a fine example his father is."

There were huge looms, and James spoke of washing and shearing, and of dyeing, carding and spinning. He showed them wool from different sheep and explained how important it was to choose the best breeds for the finished product. Sophie and Rufus felt their heads were reeling from so much information, but their teacher was passionate about his subject and obviously delighted to have an audience.

When they returned to the manor, Nancy bore Sophie off to her private withdrawing room. "I expect you have had your ear bent for long enough and would like some peace and quiet."

Sophie laughed at her grandmother and said it had been very interesting but a lot to take in all at once.

"Bless him, it's in his blood, and he can talk for hours, given the opportunity. But I've something entirely different to discuss with you. Come, sit down."

It was a room Sophie hadn't entered before. She sat on a comfortable chair with broad arms, covered in a shade of powdered pink damask that was reflected in the rest of the furniture and hangings. A woman's room. Her eye was drawn immediately to a portrait which hung over the fireplace and she couldn't help but stare at it.

Following her gaze, Nancy said, "You are right, of course. It is your mother. Your grandfather commissioned the painting before the wedding, intending it to be a gift on their first anniversary. That day never came and in any case, with things the way they were, I doubt if James would have parted with it. It has been a great comfort to me over the years."

All Sophie could say was, "But I hardly look like her, in spite of what you said! It isn't just my hair, but my features too are different from hers."

"You are right in some respects, but you must allow that I can see things you do not. There are expressions, gestures, which remind me so much of Harriet. A toss of the head, an indefinable something when you smile. As I have already told you, had I not seen the birthmark on your arm I should still have known you for my granddaughter."

Sophie could feel the love of this woman whom she'd only known for a few days, and unaccustomed rage rose in her breast. "How dared that man keep me from you my whole life? And to have deprived me of my mother's jewellery! Yes, for most of the time I would have been too young to wear it. I understand that. But it was never even shown to me. It makes me wonder what else has been held back."

"It is to be hoped you can put it behind you, my child. I carried hate in my heart for many years. It does not help and only mars precious memories. What we have missed there is no retrieving, but we have the future." She smiled broadly. "No doubt you regard me and your grandfather as very elderly but he is a robust man, and it seems to me that in the last few days I have regained something of my youth just having you by my side."

"I have seen so many changes these past few months, Grandmamma, but none has given me more happiness than finding you both." She did not mention Joseph Templeton, fairly certain that it would cause Nancy some pain, but to herself she admitted that her true father had given equal contentment. She had hoped, too, that she might have found love of her own, but since his return from Leeds Rufus had seemed a little distant. Not in any way she could analyse, but she knew things did not feel the same. She sighed and turned her attention to the lady seated opposite her.

"So, Grandmamma, tell me if you will about my mother's childhood. I have in me a certain spirit of rebellion, and I would like to think that maybe it's something I have inherited from her."

Nancy laughed. "That's for sure."

Munro and Luxton had retired to the billiards room, for the older man had no desire yet to take an afternoon nap.

"Waste of time, boy, if you ask me. I often have a game in here, now that I no longer ride. I miss it more than I can say, but don't tell the wife. She'd be reet upset if she knew."

"You don't strike me as a man who's happy to sit quietly reading, sir."

"Not unless it's accounts," James replied with a loud guffaw. "Never been bookish in my life, but if you want someone to balance the figures I'm your man." He paused, his elbow resting on the table and the cue lying across his fingertips. Then he turned his head slowly and regarded Rufus with a steady stare. "You can tell me it's none of my business, and you'd be right, but I shan't regard that. I'm a pretty observant man, and I'm as certain as I can be that your attitude towards our Sophie has altered since we last spoke on this subject. Then, if I don't mistake, you were ready to take my advice. Now you have become withdrawn. Has anything happened that you'd like to discuss with me?"

Rufus found himself liking and respecting this man even more. "You are very astute. There is something, though I'm not sure discussing it will help."

The cue was laid down and James went and leaned his back against the wall, folding his arms in front of him as he did so, and waited. Rufus adopted a similar position on the other side of the room.

"I'm not a man to denounce another, particularly in the absence of any proof, but we all have some understanding of the type of rogue Clifford has proved to be. I don't know if you're aware that Francis Follet, that's his stepson, has been trying to coerce Sophie into marriage. Several attempts were made, Follet going so far as to insinuate that she'd best take him because no-one else would have her. I know I do not betray her confidence when I tell you it was only when she saw her real father in the park that the truth came to light. She was thought not to be marriageable because of her mother's infidelity."

Munro's face turned red but he said nothing.

"We, that is my mother and I and one or two friends who are in Sophie's confidence, had all assumed he was after her fortune. She is known to be a wealthy woman, money I assume she inherited directly from her mother. Forgive me, sir, because this is as much your business as anyone's. None of us, including your granddaughter, had any inkling that upon your death she stands to inherit untold wealth. How could she when, until recently, she was not even aware of your existence? Now you have made it clear to us that you have no other kin, it comes as no surprise to me that Clifford attempted to keep Sophie hidden from the world. The man is a scoundrel, no doubt about it."

Munro moved to the table, picked up a cue and rather wildly aimed at a ball, succeeding only in tearing the baize. He flung it down again and paced the room before returning to his previous position against the wall. "And are you saying that you no longer wish to marry my granddaughter? Because of Templeton?"

"Of course not. I have been aware for some time. Indeed, I was at pains to enable them to meet each other."

"Then why have you changed your mind?"

Rufus grinned, though he was hardly amused. He pushed himself away from the wall and went to lean on the table, facing the old man across it. "I thought you would understand. I am a wealthy man, sir. A very wealthy man. Does that sound crude? It is not to my credit. Unlike you, my fortune came to me through my father, not by my own efforts. Your own is of a size that I care not even to contemplate. In marrying Sophie, I would feel it to be a very mismatched partnership. I cannot ask it of her."

The grim look that had distorted Munro's features disappeared and he broke into a smile. "And, had you been unaware of her prospects, would you then have felt mismatched, your own fortune being superior to hers?"

"Of course I wouldn't! How can you even ask such a thing?"

"Then consider what you are saying. You are prepared to sacrifice the happiness of two people for the sake of your pride. Have not enough sacrifices already been made? Do you really think Sophie would care tuppence? Tell you what, I'll leave my fortune elsewhere if it makes you happy."

"That, sir, if you'll forgive me saying so, is completely ridiculous."

"No more so than your foolish self-esteem. Enough of this, Luxton. You know what I think. Now go get her."

CHAPTER EIGHTEEN

In spite of assurances from her grandfather and the signals from Sophie, Rufus was not a man filled with confidence. For a start, she had already rejected him once. What if she turned him down again? There would be mortification for him and the possibility of embarrassment for her. The journey back into Buckinghamshire would be uncomfortable to say the very least. Nonetheless, after his talk with her grandfather he was determined to try his luck. He thought perhaps he might take her riding, but such an activity would surely have to include Caroline. And Sophie, after so long without real family, often sought the company of either Nancy or James or both. Contriving to be alone with her would not prove to be an easy task. In the end it was she and not he who brought about the opportunity for him to speak his heart. As was his habit after dinner, he was blowing a cloud outside on the terrace when she joined him.

"I thought I might find you here. I realised today and, forgive me, I cannot think why it didn't occur to me before, that I am keeping you here kicking your heels in Yorkshire when for all I know you are anxious to return to London or to Ashby."

If ever a man was being handed an opportunity on a silver platter, this was it. Diffidence must be at an end.

"I care not where I am as long as I am with you."

She looked up, quite evidently startled at his response. He pushed home his advantage.

"You must know how much I love you, Sophie. A man cannot spend time in your company and not realise what a treasure you are. I ask you, I beg you, to be my wife."

She put her hands up, to protest or not he couldn't know, but he grasped them and pulled her towards him. "Sophie, answer me. Put me out of my misery."

She stepped back and he thought he had lost. She spoke as if the words were forced from her. "You have been the best friend I have ever had. You know that, surely. When you rescued me that day, it wasn't only from an accident but from a life of oppression. We have had this conversation before, so I do not hesitate to repeat that it was the best day of my life. And since then there have been other best days. So many of them. But you cannot have thought. You are a peer of the realm and I am the misbegotten daughter of a woman with no noble blood in her veins. The world would frown upon such a union."

Relief surged through him. She hadn't said no. She had raised objections, but they were because of what she saw as her unsuitability as a bride for him. There was nothing to indicate she did not have feelings for him. On the contrary, her answer gave him hope.

"As if I should care for that! I would remind you, in any case, that your father is a member of the aristocracy. Sophie, none of these things matter if you could only find it in yourself to return my love for you."

He stepped forward again and this time she did not retreat. She looked up at him, the hint of a smile playing about the corners of her mouth. He took her face between his hands and bent to kiss her trembling lips. Then he folded her in his arms.

That is how James Munro found them a few moments later. "Well, I'm glad that's settled," he said. "Now we can all be more comfortable."

"Sir, in the absence of her father, I ask you to bestow the hand of your granddaughter upon me. I swear to honour and cherish her."

"Yes, yes, a very pretty speech, but a little late to be asking me, eh, when I find you in each other's arms." He turned to Sophie. "Come, child, let us take the news to your grandmother. I can assure you, there is no-one who will be more delighted than she."

"But I haven't said yes yet," Sophie said coyly.

"Don't you play your games off on me, miss. If what I just saw wasn't a yes, I'd like to know what is."

"Yes, Grandpapa," she replied with a meekness that fooled absolutely no-one. Rufus, the pounding of his heart now settled to a steady beat, led her back into the house, the swift glance she threw at him filling him with joy.

Naturally the wedding arrangements were the main subject for conversation. "I want everything to be done all right and tight, and I don't mind throwing my blunt at what I consider to be a good cause."

Rufus stiffened, offended at what he saw as a reflection upon himself.

Munro was quick to catch his mood. Before Luxton had a chance to respond, he added, "Now don't you get all high in the instep, young man. Think on, if you would. I've made a lot of mistakes in my time, and none greater than the sacrifice of my only daughter to a man I wouldn't give the time of day to nowadays. I don't want to get it wrong this time."

He sounded almost plaintive and Rufus relaxed, realising how important it was to this venerable old gentleman. "The decision must be Sophie's, of course," said her betrothed, "but it would be my dearest wish for us to be married in the family chapel at Ashby. I know my mother would feel the same."

Nancy, with her small frame but considerably large personality, was the next to speak. "I'll not have you spoiling things, James Munro. It will be as our Sophie wishes. Then maybe she and her new husband might come and pay us a visit after the wedding."

Sophie and Rufus looked at each other in astonishment, he being the first to recover.

"No, Mrs Munro. Sir. You mistake. Sophie will not be married without the support of her grandparents. You will come and stay at Ashby. If you feel able to make the journey, I will come into Yorkshire myself to escort you back. It matters not how long it takes and we can rest on alternate days if necessary, so that it doesn't prove to be too arduous."

The relief of the two was plain to see as their shoulders relaxed and they smiled.

"Grandmamma, you cannot have thought I would be married without you?" Sophie hesitated a moment. "There is one other thing, though." She was treading as softly as she could, but this was something that had to be said. "Naturally I shall want my father there to give me away. I know that when he was a young man there was no love lost between you, but I am as much a part of him as I am of you. After all these years it would be sad to see any animosity between you."

Munro looked at his wife. "There will be none from us. We can only hope he has it in him to forgive us for the half a lifetime of pain which we were responsible for inflicting upon him. Nay, lass," he said as Sophie raised her hand in protest, "it's the truth after all. I was that used to giving orders and having them obeyed that I failed to see the damage we were doing, even with our Harriet's pleas. We thought her just a young girl with an infatuation we were certain would pass. It's Templeton as may not want to have anything to do with us. You may condemn us, but no-one has more contempt for my actions back then than I do myself."

Nancy was softly crying and Sophie went to her. Rufus, on the other hand, spoke quietly to Munro. "You spoke to me recently of misplaced pride. Will you now let your own pride stand in the way of your granddaughter's happiness? I can assure you she will not be happy if she thinks you and Mrs Munro to be forever dwelling on the past. What's done is done. Nothing can change that. You can either let it colour your future or you can be joyful that you have regained something you thought lost forever. Which is it to be, sir?"

For some minutes James Munro had looked to be his age, and smaller somehow. These words, however, touched his sense of humour, never far from the surface, and he drew himself up to his full height once more. "Not shy of giving me my own, then, are you? I can foresee many lively conversations between us, Luxton, but they will not be on the journey south. Mrs Munro and me, we can travel without an escort, thank you very much, and I expect you to be busy at Ashby making all in readiness for the finest wedding there ever was. So what do you think of that!"

"I think, sir, that you are a complete hand. And whatever else I think I would not dream of saying to you under your own roof," he said, laughing and shaking the old man's hand.

Sophie and Rufus left Yorkshire two days later. Inevitably it took a long time to reach Buckinghamshire, but the necessity of travelling slowly was no hardship to a couple who were happy to spend every waking moment in each other's company. Caroline was grateful that she need not feel guilty about their slow progress and, as a consequence, all three reached Ashby in a relaxed frame of mind. The perfect companion, Miss Ward excused herself almost immediately upon their arrival, leaving the way clear for Sophie and Rufus to tell his mother their news without delay.

"Mama, I have some wonderful news to impart which I hope will please you. Sophie has done me the honour of accepting my proposal. We are to be married here at Ashby, in the chapel."

If he had thought to surprise Lady Luxton, he was sadly disappointed. "My dearest children, I couldn't be happier. It has been my cherished wish for some time now that you would make a match, for I never saw two people more suited. Augusta Bridlington thought exactly the same."

"You have been discussing us with Lady Bridlington?" Rufus said, trying to sound cross but unable to stop himself smiling. He'd carried hope in his heart for so long that it was a relief to allow his feelings to show.

"Is it to take place soon? A summer wedding would be lovely. But you haven't yet told me, Sophie. How were you received in Halifax? Were your grandparents accepting of the situation? Will they come?"

"Stop, Mama! So many questions all at once. First and most important, all is well with the Munros. They were in a fair way to making up for lost time when we had to leave and will come whenever we summon them. Sophie and I have agreed that we would like our marriage to take place as soon as possible, but as yet her father is unaware of our betrothal and we don't know if he has returned from Scotland to his lodgings in London."

"I am to write to him today, Elizabeth, in the hope that I will find him sooner rather than later, for I would not like our engagement to be made public until he has first been contacted. All our plans must wait upon his response. In the meantime, I will return with Caroline to Rose Cottage. How glad I am that I decided to purchase a house in this county. At least we will be able, all of us, to see each other, if not every day then certainly often. It may be some time before I hear from my father and there is much to do in the meantime."

"Will you stay a few days to recover before you go home?" Elizabeth asked. "Do you plan to go to London to purchase your trousseau? I would be delighted if you would permit me to help you. I well remember the delights we had shopping for Lydia."

Rufus, deciding that the conversation was moving out of his domain, excused himself and left the two women together. It was later when he and Sophie were talking quietly in the withdrawing room, waiting for Elizabeth and Caroline to join them, that he realised his betrothed was deeply disturbed about something.

"What is it, my darling? I can see you are upset."

She smiled, a vain effort for the result was wan. "Earlier, when I was speaking to your mother, she told me it was her intention to remove to the dower house."

"It is customary under the circumstances."

"I will not have it!"

Rufus put his hand to her head and ran his fingers through her curls. "I have noted before that you have a temper to match your flaming hair. May I ask what you suggest instead?"

She flung his hand away, her feelings getting the better of her. "I was sure you would understand. Think back to when you both took me into your home. I stayed here for several weeks in perfect harmony with you all. Why cannot the same thing happen after we are married? Elizabeth has stood as a mother to me these many months now. Would you turn your mother out? I cannot. I will not."

Rufus enfolded her in his arms. Rigid at first, he felt the tension leave her body as she began to relax. He murmured into ear, assuring her that he would do whatever she wished. "But if you can persuade her, I for one will be surprised."

"Then we must do so together, for I could never forgive myself for driving her out of her home."

It would be hard, he knew that. On the one hand his bride was declaring she would not move from her position, and his mother, he was well aware, would be as adamant that she must follow convention.

"One thing is for sure, Sophie. Life with you will not be boring."

In the end it was Caroline Ward who held the key to resolving the difference between Sophie and Elizabeth, neither of whom was prepared to move from her standpoint. Lady Luxton hit upon the solution.

"You seem to enjoy living in the country, Caroline. My understanding is that before you joined Sophie you were residing in Bath, do I have that right?"

"I was, and I count myself very lucky to have seen her advertisement. I know there are those who entertain the conviction that town life is superlative, but for me the freedom of movement and fresh air outweigh any advantages the access to amenities might have. I'm sure I don't know what I shall do once Sophie and Lord Luxton are married, for nothing is more certain than that she will no longer require my services." She stopped abruptly, her hand covering her mouth in her discomfiture, aware that her plight and the countess's sympathetic nature had provoked her into betraying her inner feelings. "I beg your pardon. Please, do not to consider my concerns, nor mention them to Sophie, for she has enough on her mind at present. Forget what I said. No doubt I shall come about."

Elizabeth felt nothing but compassion for this young woman. "I shall of course honour your wishes, Caroline, but I'm wondering if we might, the two of us, be able to help each other. Sophie has the kindest nature, but I have recently discovered in her a stubborn streak which I am finding it difficult to overcome." Her broad smile took the sting out of her words and she continued on. "You may know that she is determined I shall remain at Ashby after she and my son are wed. While I honour her for such sentiments, she is blind to my own wishes. When I married the earl, my son's father, he had not yet succeeded to the title. His own sire was widowed and lived with us here, or rather we with him, until his demise. It was no way to go on, for they argued incessantly and that in itself prevented me from developing what could have been a very comfortable relationship with my father-in-law. There is no way I would so risk jeopardising what Sophie and I have found together. In any case, the dower house will suit me admirably. I am strongly of the opinion that she thinks I would be lonely. How would it be then if, upon their marriage, you move to become my companion? I should be very happy to have you, you know." Caroline folded and unfolded her hands several times, prompting Elizabeth to continue, "You do not like the idea? Don't be embarrassed. I perfectly understand that you would wish to be with a younger woman than I. We shall say no more about it."

"No, you misunderstand. It isn't that at all. I should be honoured and delighted. How could I not be? But I feel you have been manoeuvred into making an offer you might regret."

Elizabeth was at pains to reassure her, and so it was that when Sophie began to look mulish when the subject next arose her mama-in-law was able to put forward a perfectly plausible solution. She supported her case by repeating the same story she had told Caroline. "I would be mortified if we should be at outs, you and I. We are, both of us, strong-minded women and, with your new-found independence, I make no doubt you would want to be the mistress of your own home. And how do you think that would sit? For a start, the poor servants would not know to whom they should go with their queries. Who would be placed where at the table? Whose decision would it be to approve the weekly menu? Authorise new purchases to the housekeeper? You see," she said, pressing home her advantage as Sophie began to giggle at the ridiculousness of the situation. "An establishment can have only one mistress. The dower house is a delightful building, and I shall be very comfortable there. Let us talk no more about it, for I would rather be discussing our trip to London."

Rufus, when he joined them later, was delighted to perceive that the tension which had been recently present had dissipated, and talk was instead of the proposed expedition to purchase bridal clothes.

CHAPTER NINETEEN

Sophie was first to return to Rose Cottage and await her father's reply to her letter.

"It is to be hoped that it won't be long before you hear. It has been some weeks now since Templeton journeyed into Scotland. I don't believe he had the intention of making a prolonged visit," Rufus said as he escorted her and Caroline to Cholesbury. "In the meantime I hope you will not tire of me, for I am determined to ride over as often as I can. I dare say my mother will be pleased to be rid of me, for I have seen more of her these past six months than the previous six years."

"I suspect she will not tire of you so easily."

There were things they wished to discuss, but in a closed carriage with Miss Ward for company it was not the time. Rufus remained overnight, promising to return as soon as he was able.

Sophie wrote to her grandparents.

I cannot tell you enough how happy you have made me. I am anxious to see you again as soon as possible but fear we must wait now until arrangements have been made for the wedding. Thus far I have not had a reply from my father, but as soon as that is to hand I shall write again when I hope to have clearer details of what will happen next. In the meantime, I remain your loving and affectionate Sophie.

When days turned to weeks with no response from her father, it was evident to her betrothed that Sophie was becoming increasingly distressed. He sought to reassure her.

"Would it help if I went to town to see what I might discover? You will know from what I have told you about Edward Boyle that there are things I should discuss that I am often only too happy to leave to him. He is a superlative agent and is at present in London at my behest. Perhaps your letter has gone astray. I will call on your father and ask his permission in person, a courtesy I should in any case extend to him."

"Oh, would you?" Sophie said, her hands clasping his, her eyes expressing her relief that something was to be done. "It's foolish of me, I know, but it seems unlike him not to have replied. But of course you may well be right and he has received nothing from me."

"If it will help to comfort you, I am only too happy to go. My only reservation is that it will be many days before I see you again. In the meantime, try if you can to spend some time riding with Caroline. Between her and Snowflake it should rid you of the fidgets I can see are threatening to overwhelm you. I shall leave first thing in the morning," he said, kissing first one hand and then the other before relinquishing them. He left immediately after breakfast and, taking his advice, she went for a good gallop.

The earl reached town that same evening, having stopped on the way only to enjoy a pint of ale and some cold meats. Driving his curricle and not pushing his team, he was able to complete the journey without a change of horses. Stopping at Solgrave House to put off his driving cape and clothes, he dressed and went to his club to dine. It was thin of company as many people had already left for the summer, but he found Lord Bridlington in one of the card rooms.

"You're lucky to have caught me. Emily and I are taking my mother into the country tomorrow. I am only here this evening because they were discussing some last-minute arrangements and my presence was obviously neither required nor wanted. 'Do go to your club, Oliver,' Mama commanded, so naturally I did not need telling twice. Haven't seen you in a while. How did you and Miss Clifford go on in Yorkshire? Is all right and tight with her grandparents?"

"It is, and I want you to wish me happy, Ollie. Sophie has done me the honour of agreeing to become my wife."

"Well, thank goodness for that. Not before time, either. Congratulations, old man. I couldn't be happier for you."

Rufus asked him not to say anything, as no announcement was to be made before Templeton was made aware of the situation. "It's the reason I'm in town, actually. Sophie wrote to him but has received no reply. I've come to see if I can run him to ground. Have you seen him recently?"

"Not since before I last saw you. Wasn't he travelling to some godforsaken place to see friends?"

"He was, but he should have been back long before now."

Rufus was beginning to feel concerned. He visited Templeton's lodgings first thing the next morning. There was no response to his second rap of the knocker and he was just about to turn away, thinking his prey had perhaps gone for an early morning ride, when the door opened to reveal a very harassed-looking man who was of a similar age to his quarry. He had seen him before, some time ago, on the first occasion he had visited the lodgings to arrange for father and daughter to meet properly for the first time. John Drummond, he knew, had served Templeton for several years. He appeared quite different now. Worried, distraught almost.

"What is it, man? Has something happened to your master?"

"That it has, my lord. But come in and I'll tell you all."

Rufus swept past him, more apprehensive than he had been in a long while. He flung his hat and gloves on the stand in the hall and said again, more urgently this time, "What is it? Where is Mr Templeton?"

"In his bed and lucky to be alive, sir. Nigh on a month ago now, it happened. Set upon, we were, on Finchley Common, on our way back from Scotland. Someone fired off his barker and before we knew it the driver had drawn to a halt and two villains pulled open the doors of the coach. Well, my master is no coward, nor me neither, my lord, but we'd have handed over our money without a struggle. Only sensible thing to do when you're staring down the barrel of a gun. Only they weren't after money, oh no. 'This is our man,' said one to the other, and then blow me down he shot Mr Templeton. Close to him as you are to me now. I did what I could to stem the blood, but it was flowing that fast I couldn't stop it. The two men, they just took off. The master's travelling box was there, plain enough to see, but they weren't interested in that. Murder's what was on their minds and murder they committed, near as, dammit."

"He's still alive, you said?"

"He is, sir. I'll take you to him now, shall I?"

The man lying on the bed was barely recognisable as the robust adventurer Rufus had seen only a few weeks ago. Only the colour of his hair gave him away. Even with the covers over him Rufus could tell he'd lost a considerable amount of weight. He was dreadfully weak, but he was conscious and had retained his sense of humour.

"Forgive me if I don't rise to greet you, Luxton. As you can see, I'm not quite myself at the moment."

"You've seen the doctor?"

"That butcher! Yes, though I told Drummond not to let him in again after he'd mauled me about so badly. Still, he took the bullet out at least, so that's a blessing. Only I was out of my mind for a while and Drummond didn't listen. Just as well, I suppose. And the doctor told him what to do for me. I'd be a dead man now if not."

"He told me it wasn't a robbery. That they meant to kill you."

Templeton grimaced as he moved unguardedly. "Not a doubt about it. Once the driver had stopped shaking, Drummond ordered him to bring me back here as fast as possible. By that time I was unconscious and all John could do was put as much pressure on the wound as he was able to prevent me bleeding to death. Don't know how he managed it but here I am, alive to tell the tale."

"Do you have any idea who would do such a thing?"

"I can think of only one person who hates me enough to want to take my life, but I've no proof. Probably thinks he's succeeded too. I don't believe he'd come to town to check, and not a soul but the doctor has seen me since."

In spite of his host's attempt at humour, Rufus could see he'd used up all his reserves relating the tale and was exhausted. Saying he would return later in the day, he left him to recover as best he could. Out in the hall he asked Drummond if he thought his master was fit to travel. When he heard Luxton wanted to take him to his daughter in Buckinghamshire, he said the wound had healed enough not to open up and that in a well-sprung carriage with a careful driver it might be possible to transfer him. He was of the opinion that nothing would be more beneficial than for him to see Miss Clifford.

"Then we must see if it can be arranged, and speedily. You'll travel with your master? I'll drive myself, though I'll need to hire a suitable carriage. I came in my curricle, but my tiger can see that it's returned to Ashby. I'll make what arrangements I can this afternoon and return here later in the day. I'm hoping we'll be able to leave in the morning. Have I forgotten anything?"

"No sir, not that I can think of. Right glad I am to have you in charge, my lord, if you don't mind me saying so. Will it suit you for me to tell him what's happening?"

"Certainly."

"Then I make no doubt we'll see an improvement straight away. Fretting about Miss Sophie, he's been. Now we'll be all right and tight."

Rufus wished he had as much faith in himself as this man so obviously did and went off to put his plans in place.

Rufus returned to the lodgings later in the afternoon bearing the doctor with him.

"It's of no use you arguing," Luxton told Templeton when he protested. "If you wish me to convey you to Miss Clifford, you will do as you are told. I will not take the responsibility of moving you without this man's consent, so you may as well give in gracefully. I shall wait outside while he examines you."

It was some time before the door opened, but the news was positive.

"The wound has healed well and a very nice job my colleague has made of it. What needs to be done now is for the gentleman's strength to be built up, for he is as weak as can be. My understanding is that you are to take him into the country. Best thing for him in my opinion, particularly at this season. Got someone to look after him, have you? Get some decent food inside him. None of these gruels. He has a large frame and it needs filling out."

"Thank you, doctor. I am taking him to his daughter. She is a practical young woman who will stand no nonsense from him. I appreciate you coming at such short notice."

"Not at all. Don't hesitate to call in the local man if you feel the need, but I'm confident he will do better with his daughter in charge than languishing here in his bed. Good day to you, sir."

With his concerns laid to rest, Rufus told Drummond to have his master ready early the next morning. It was his intention to complete the journey in one day, normally easy enough but, with an invalid in the carriage and a determination to avoid every hole in the road, it would be a harder than usual task. So it was that none saw Joseph Templeton's departure from London and, as he had not left the house since the attack, he had to all intents and purposes disappeared.

CHAPTER TWENTY

The journey was a trial for Sophie's father. By the time they arrived at Rose Cottage he looked even worse than when Rufus had first seen him and, having checked on his passenger from time to time, he was beginning to doubt the wisdom of having moved him.

Being summer, it was still light when they reached their destination. Sophie, hearing the noise of a carriage from where she sat with Caroline in the withdrawing room, stood to look out of the window. Seeing Rufus at the reins, she ran outside. He'd had no time to write and warn her of what was to come, so he jumped down and gripped her hands. Looking earnestly into her eyes, he said, "I fear you are in for a bit of a shock. I have Joseph with me, but he is in bad frame, though I had the doctor's consent to bring him to you. Go and organise a room for him, if you will, and I shall carry him there. I'll tell you all once he is settled."

Sophie didn't waste any time arguing or even peering into the coach but turned on her heel and raced back into the house. By the time Rufus had carried Templeton upstairs, the window had been opened a little to allow some air into the room, the covers had been turned down and a candle lit on the bedside table. Joseph smiled wanly at his daughter but was unable to do more as he was laid exhausted on the bed.

"Don't distress yourself, Papa. Get some rest now and we will talk in the morning. You cannot know how happy I am to see you." She stroked the red hair back from his forehead and left the room to find John Drummond waiting outside in the corridor. "You are my father's man, are you not? Lord Luxton will tell me all, but in the meantime I would be grateful if you would consent to stay with your master through the night. I shall have some food brought up for you and a truckle bed set up so that you may get some sleep."

"I did my best for him, miss, and I won't leave him now, not after all the years we've been together."

It was evident he was choked up with emotion and himself on the point of exhaustion. Sophie reassured him and almost pushed him into the room in her anxiety to join Rufus, who had gone downstairs to wait for her. He jumped up when she entered.

"I gather my father has been in some sort of accident or suffered a severe illness. I will not ask questions. Just tell it to me as it is, if you would, without embellishment or concern for my feelings. I shall not faint, I promise."

She was indeed shocked when she learned how Templeton had sustained his injury. Rufus made no mention of his suspicion as to who might be the perpetrator. He told her of the doctor's visit and that, as bad as he looked, her father was on the mend. "And you are to feed him well and build him up so that he can stand strong at your side on our wedding day," he added, trying to lighten the atmosphere a little. "Not that he knows about it yet. Your letter lay unopened with the rest, for Drummond did not consider him in any state to be dealing with correspondence and naturally he did not recognise your hand. I have brought everything with me. Have you dined yet? I could eat a whole side of beef, for I've had nothing all day. Drummond too will need something."

"I have, but I shall sit with you while you eat. If I know anything of Caroline, she will already have given instructions. Poor Drummond looked fit to drop and you, sir, do not look much better, if you will permit me to say so."

"And you, my darling, are a sight for sore eyes. May I have a bed for the night? It is far too late for me to be setting out for Ashby, and in any case you might need help with your father."

"That too I am certain Caroline will have organised."

"In that case there is nothing left for me to do than to kiss you, the thought of which I can tell you has been sustaining me these many miles."

Later, when Miss Ward had retired and they were still sitting at the table, Sophie judged it time to ask Rufus the questions which had been building up in her mind, foremost amongst which was why would anyone fire at a man without stealing his possessions? Rufus did not prevaricate, though he had anticipated the look of horror on her face when told that someone had deliberately set out to commit murder.

"But why?"

This question was harder to answer, but in the end he decided that only the truth as he and Templeton saw it would serve. The colour fled from Sophie's cheeks and it took her some moments to digest fully what he was saying.

"You will know that there is no love lost between myself and the baron, but I can understand why he would hate my father. No man, no matter how objectionable, could easily accept that his new wife, coerced into marriage or not, had been unfaithful to him and had borne her lover's child. But to carry such vindictiveness for twenty-one years, and to resort to murder! I find it hard to believe."

Rufus agreed that he would not have carried out such a deed himself. "But he might have engaged another to do his dirty work for him."

"Francis! You think it was Francis who pulled the trigger?"

"Just think of the circumstances. Follet has been raised to believe that one day you would be his wife and he would have access to untold wealth, if not immediately then certainly upon the death of your grandparents. There can be no other reason for you being kept in the dark as to their existence. You have rejected him many times. He has been scorned and robbed of his dream by you, my darling. Not only does Clifford hate your father, but Follet must now feel the same way about you. Killing Templeton would be a way for both to achieve vengeance." He smiled at her gently as several emotions chased each other across her face, anger being the overriding one.

"What a loathsome thing to have done. How could he!"

"Remember, we have no proof. All is as yet conjecture. Now, before I retire I shall look in upon your father, and tomorrow I must write to my mother. I am not leaving here until our patient is on the mend, even if I have to sleep in the stable with Snowflake."

He was rewarded with a smile. "No doubt she would enjoy that, but with both my father and Caroline to chaperone me I think it acceptable that you remain in the house. I wish you a good night's sleep. And," she added as they both rose from the table and she raised her hand to his cheek, "my heartfelt thanks for all you have done. Once more Lord Luxton has come to my rescue."

Joseph Templeton awoke in a strange room with no clear idea of how he had got there. Deplorably weak but otherwise none the worse for his travels, he tried to sit up. Drummond was beside him in a moment.

"Stay where you are, sir."

"And where exactly am I, John?"

"You are at Rose Cottage, and if you promise to lay quietly I'll fetch Miss Sophie to you."

Immediately he ceased struggling and watched the door intently as John left, his gaze never wavering until his daughter came to his bedside. She stroked the hair back from his forehead in much the same way as she had the previous evening, then dropped a kiss where it had been and pulled up a chair to sit beside him.

"I hear you have been having some unpleasant adventures, Papa," she said lightly, hoping to set the mood for, though the situation was grave indeed, now was not the time to be discussing it.

He responded in kind, glad to be holding Sophie's hand. She had been in his thoughts both when conscious and even in his delirium. He hadn't believed he would survive to see her again. "Ha! I fear unpleasant doesn't sufficiently describe it, but one glance at your fair face and all is right again."

"Perhaps not quite that. You are reduced to skin and bone, and I have ordered breakfast to be brought to you. It is my intention to sit here until you have finished every morsel, and you needn't think I will take no for an answer. I didn't inherit your red hair for nothing, you know."

Both smiled and looked up at a knock on the door.

"Come in, John, come in, for I fear I am going to be bullied and need your support."

Drummond set the tray he was carrying on top of a chest of drawers and helped his master into a sitting position before retrieving the board and placing it across Joseph's legs. The support when he gave it, however, was given not to Templeton but to Sophie and between bullying and coaxing they managed to persuade their patient to eat most of his breakfast before exhaustion overcame him.

"It is time for you to rest again, Papa. I shall return later when you have recovered a little."

He gripped her hand. "Promise me."

She smiled, her eyes full of tenderness. "Even Snowflake shall not keep me away, though it is my intention to ride while you are asleep. I will send Bertha to sit with you so that John may stretch his legs and perhaps himself have a proper sleep. I don't consider you to be in danger, but we will none of us leave you alone. That I can most certainly promise you."

He was content and fell asleep almost before she had left the room.

She found Rufus addressing a hearty breakfast and sat down to report on her father's progress, the smile still playing around her lips.

"He is too weak as yet to be belligerent, but I fear we shall have a struggle on our hands as he grows stronger. In the meantime, John and I will feed him up as much as we can. It is to be hoped this fine weather continues and we will soon be able to take him out into the sunshine, if you don't mind carrying him. It will be some time before he is fit enough to walk unaided."

"May I suggest that you move your father down to the library? With all the toing and froing that I anticipate it will be easier for all concerned if he is on this level. It will be easy enough to have a bed made up in there and then, when he is well enough, it will be more convenient for him to join us in the drawing room or outside in the garden."

"What a splendid idea, my love. I shall see to it now before I change into my riding habit. Would you care to join me?"

"If you have a horse large enough to take me, I shall be delighted. You must remember I came in my curricle. Which reminds me, Wilfred should be here later today. I told him to break his journey overnight in order not to push my team."

"Well, as you said when first we viewed this place, there is ample accommodation in the stables. Rufus, would you mind if Caroline joins us? Riding is her greatest pleasure and I feel it would be churlish of me to deny her, even though I would wish to be alone with you."

Impulsively he went to hug her shoulders.

"What was that for?"

"Because you are the kindest, most thoughtful person I know. Of course I don't mind. And, though I would wish for the circumstances to be different, there will be sufficient opportunity for us to be private in the coming days. If you are agreeable, I would like to tell your father of our betrothal as soon as possible."

"It is my wish also, but I should like to wait until he has regained some of his strength, though I am certain he will be delighted and the news will do him no harm."

"Sophie, Sophie, I cannot wait for you to be my wife."

"Then we must do what we can to hasten my father's return to health, for it cannot be till then."

Later that day Rufus went to visit Templeton in order to carry him downstairs to the library, which had by then been made ready for him.

"I'm afraid I've come to maul you about again, sir, but it has been decided that it will be more convenient all round if you are taken to the library where we will have easier access to you."

"I hate being so incapacitated," Joseph said, trying and failing to raise himself onto his elbows.

"Better then to give yourself the time you need to mend rather than rush to do what you are unable to. You are lucky to be alive, you know. It will be better in the end if you submit now," Rufus said kindly.

"Very well, but before you move me I would tell you more of what happened if you have a mind to listen."

Rufus pulled up a chair. "Certainly I will. Have you remembered any more details above those you have already shared with me?"

"Nothing new, but I have been mulling over what happened. I have had plenty of time to do so, after all. You may not be aware that Follet holds a minor title. Inherited from his father and pretty much all he inherited. His mother was lucky to have caught Clifford, for she brought no dowry with her and we know how he feels about money. Perhaps he felt the need to provide a mother for Sophie, who knows? But this is my point. When I was set upon, it became almost immediately obvious that being passive was going to serve no purpose. I flung out my hands in an attempt to grab my assailant, even as the shot was fired. I fell back and knew nothing more, for days as it turned out. But John found something clasped in my fist. It was a button and the vanity of the man had caused him to have his arms engraved upon it. I can tell you, Luxton, that the button belonged to Francis Follet!"

Templeton fell back onto the pillows, his effort at putting such a speech together having exhausted him. Rufus gave him time to recover, saying he would return later to take him downstairs. Finding Drummond outside, he enquired if he had brought the evidence to Buckinghamshire. Receiving confirmation, he asked that it be handed into his care.

"I shall fetch it now, sir."

Rufus took it straight to Sophie, who looked questioningly at him as she had expected him to be carrying her father.

"He has been talking to me and tired himself out. I will bring him down later. But first I want you to see this."

In his palm rested a large and somewhat ornate button, the coat of arms clear to see on its surface. Sophie's hand went to her throat, sufficient reaction to satisfy him that she recognised it for what it was.

"It is one of a set of six. I sewed them on myself, so I cannot be mistaken. This belongs to my stepbrother. You had it from my father?"

"He grabbed it as he was shot at. There can be no doubt, then. Follet, and perhaps Clifford too, were prepared to commit murder."

Sophie paced up and down in agitation. She stopped and looked at him for a moment before continuing and it was clear she was running everything over in her mind. Finally she sank into a chair, worn down by the emotion of it all. It was a sad face that she presented to Rufus as she looked up at him, standing quietly by the fireplace and waiting for her to be ready.

"It is difficult to accept that a man I have grown up with could resort to such an act. I have never liked him, but this is something else. Why do you think he would have taken an accomplice with him, and who might it have been?"

"Hard to know, but it is to be hoped he hasn't been in the habit of committing such deeds. Perhaps he merely hired someone to hold up the coach. We may never know. I am as certain as I can be that Clifford himself would not have taken part. In fact, I have revised my previous opinion and think in all probability that he would not even have been aware of his stepson's plot to kill your father. It was too hazardous. If he were to stoop to such baseness, he would have engaged some other villain rather than permit Follet to risk his life. The baron may be lacking in many ways, but I think we can exonerate him from this crime."

"What are we to do? Should we confront Francis, do you think?"

"What I think is that we should wait until your father is recovered sufficiently to discuss it with him. He is the victim in this and his must be the decision."

She had to agree with him, though it irked her to have to remain inactive when she was so anxious to see the perpetrator brought to justice. How different she was now from the submissive young woman she had been before being thrown from her horse.

CHAPTER TWENTY-ONE

Wilfred had arrived during the afternoon and Rufus announced his intention of taking Sophie for a drive the following day so that they might explore the surrounding countryside.

"And now you may legitimately rest your head upon my shoulder," he said with a smile. He could see that she was looking puzzled and remembered that he had never described to her that first drive when he had needed to support her unconscious form while taking her back to Ashby. He recounted the story to her now.

"Just as well I did not know. I should have been outraged," she laughed. "Though I can admit to you now, sir, that it wasn't very long before I would have done much to feel the comfort of your arm about me. No, stay where you are," she said as he moved impulsively towards her. "We have too much to talk about to engage in such frivolity."

"Frivolity!"

"Yes, my love, frivolity. Now, if you would be so kind as to return to my father's room, I would be glad to see him settled into the library."

He went, threatening to claim his reward later, and by the time Templeton had been moved to his new quarters the day was well advanced. Nothing more was said of the attack, though both went to sit with him for a while after supper. Instead, not so ill that he didn't perceive the look that passed between Sophie and Rufus, he demanded, "What's all this then?"

So the truth was out and Rufus formally begged him for his daughter's hand in marriage.

"Don't you come the sweet with me, young man. As if what I say would make any difference. You are clearly besotted with each other and nothing I might assert would serve any purpose. Not that I would say anything. I am more delighted than I can tell you."

There was another hurdle to be crossed and Sophie leapt it nimbly. "We have already gained the blessing of my grandparents. They are to journey south when a date is fixed for the wedding and they are looking forward to seeing you after all these years."

"Don't you try and cut a sham with me, young lady. As if they would want to have anything to do with me."

She was quick to detect the anger in his voice and sought to reassure him. "You are wrong, Papa. Their attitude is much changed and they have nothing but regret for their actions all those years ago. They are hoping you can find it in you to forgive them for what they did to you and to my mother." She knelt by his bed and took his hand in hers. "It is the truth, I promise you. They have lived for twenty-two years with a terrible guilt. I hope you can accept their remorse, for it is genuine. And," she smiled, "I would hate to see my father and grandparents at odds. I have waited a lifetime for you all and I will allow nothing to adversely affect my happiness in this regard." She was pleased to see him settle back against the pillows again. His heightened colour had subsided and he was calm.

"Very well. So tell me, when is this wedding to take place?"

"That depends on you, sir," said Rufus. "Sophie will be content with nothing less than walking down the aisle on her father's arm, so you must see how important it is to me that you recover as quickly as possible."

"In that case, I suggest you both leave me in peace so I can get some rest. Come and see me again tomorrow, Luxton, and we will discuss settlements."

"That will not be necessary, sir. You cannot offer me any treasure that is greater than your daughter."

The next morning Rufus drove Sophie in the direction of Wendover, the reins in one hand as he flung his free arm carelessly about her shoulders. He began to whistle, much as he had on the day he encountered her lying by the roadside. She looked sideways at him and smiled.

"It is gratifying to know that you are so relaxed in my company you do not feel the need to observe the usual conventions." He stopped mid-tune, startled for a moment into silence. "You were whistling."

"Was I? It's an unconscious thing with me. It happens only when I am most content. I beg you will forgive my bad manners."

"You, sir, have no shame. But while I have your attention, will you not glance about you for a moment? The country around here is extraordinarily beautiful, is it not?"

"The most beautiful thing is right beside me but yes, the aspect is particularly pleasing and it is good that we seem to have the road to ourselves."

At that moment another carriage appeared around the bend, coming towards them at a greater speed than was appropriate. Sophie had the gratification of seeing Rufus, in one fluid movement, snatch back his arm, take the reins in both hands and perform a manoeuvre of which any member of the Four Horse Club would have been proud, notwithstanding the fact that he was driving only a pair. The carriages passed each other without mishap and Sophie and Rufus glanced back to see the other driver shaking his fist at them as though the fault had been theirs. Laughing so much that he had to draw his horses to a halt, Rufus, when he had recovered sufficiently, took Sophie's hand in his and kissed her fingertips.

"With your permission, as soon as we return to Rose Cottage it is my intention to send an announcement of our betrothal to the *Morning Post*. Your father is aware of our engagement. There can be no further objection, nor any reason for delay. I shall register the banns and we must hope that Templeton's recovery progresses speedily, for I desire nothing more than to make you my wife as soon as may be."

Still bubbling with laughter herself, Sophie could find no objection to this proposal. She felt a deep contentment when she was with this man and knew that it would always be so, for there was a meeting of minds as well as of hearts. "And I shall write to your mother and beg her to come and stay for a while. I should not blame her at all if she feels that we have deserted her. Lydia is now with Freddie, and you have been in Cholesbury for some time. While you are never continuously at Ashby, she certainly always enjoyed the company of your sister. I only hope she does not consider herself to have been neglected. In any case," she added, with a simplicity that made him long to take her once more into his arms, "I miss her."

"In that case, I shall turn my curricle around at the next opportunity, hoping that we don't encounter another reckless driver in the process, and return home."

As they drove back, she discussed with him the advisability of writing also to her grandparents. While there was more than sufficient room to accommodate them at Rose Cottage, they were unsure as yet how long her father's recovery would take. Neither deemed it a good idea to ask such an elderly couple, no matter how fit they might be, to come first to Cholesbury and thereafter remove to Ashby for the wedding. They knew nothing of the attempt on Templeton's life and it would be bound to come to light if they arrived during the period of his convalescence. All things considered, it was decided that they should remain in Yorkshire until such time as their plans were more firmly in place.

"I shall nonetheless write to them, for it has been a while since I last did so."

"I am, as ever, in agreement with you."

Sophie gurgled. "What a fib. When you know you delight in crossing swords with me at every opportunity."

"Sophie," Rufus said warningly, "if I were not holding the reins I would, I would … well, I expect you know what I would."

"But holding the reins you are," she said, with no little regret.

Upon their return to Rose Cottage, both went to the library to fulfil their allotted tasks. Joseph, while he appreciated the company, sat up in bed reading a book, not wishing to disturb them. His inactivity was beginning to irk him and, when both had laid down their pens, he asked if he might not be taken out into the garden to enjoy the sunshine.

"Indeed you may. John Drummond is fashioning some sort of bath chair for you and it is to be hoped you may soon acquire a degree of independence. In the meantime, if you should not object, I shall this time carry you out myself, after which I will go in search of him and see how close he is to completing his task."

Rufus joined Sophie and her father again not many minutes later, triumphantly pushing a chair to which wheels had been attached, and Joseph made his first attempt to use it. Sophie's heart was in her mouth, but Rufus stood by in case it threatened to turn over. No such mishap occurred and Joseph sat back, tired but satisfied, and assured them he would not much longer be such a burden to them.

"You could never be that, Papa, but it will be good to see you getting about again. I wonder, have you decided how you might like to proceed against Francis? I cannot bear that he is walking around a free man after what he tried to do to you."

"That was my initial reaction, I must confess, but what purpose would it serve once more to be dragging our name through the mud, Sophie? He has failed, and I cannot see him making another attempt. I had more than enough grief from Clifford and his family when your mother was alive. I prefer to let the matter rest. Now that I have found you I shall not lose you again but, after travelling the world for most of my adult life, I discover in myself a reluctance to settle in one place. Once you and Luxton here have tied the knot I may leave you with impunity, safe in the knowledge that you are in his care. I shall not stay away for such an extended period of time as before, but neither can I remain."

Rufus agreed it was best to let the matter drop but Sophie, who had spent a lifetime under the same roof as the perpetrator, could not find it in herself to forgive, or indeed to forget, quite so easily. She accepted that it was not her decision to make but put her head in her hand and pouted.

"Why such a face, young lady?"

She laughed, a delightful sound that drew a smile from her companions. "Well, you see, if your recovery is hastened, so must then be my wedding, which naturally I am eager for. However, it would also mean the expedition of your departure, for which I am not so eager. You must see what a difficult position you put me in, surely."

Three days later Joseph had become almost entirely self-sufficient and all that remained was for him to regain his former strength. Elizabeth Solgrave arrived at Rose Cottage and arrangements for the forthcoming nuptials began in earnest. Rufus declared that he would have to return to Ashby within the week, for there was much to prepare. In the meantime, invitations were ordered and Sophie and her mama-in-law spent a pleasant afternoon, having between them drawn up a list, in directing and having them despatched. At some point it was decided that the whole party would travel together, there being no further need to remain at Rose Cottage, and Sophie knew that in a way she would be sad to leave, for she wouldn't return. These last few weeks had been the happiest she had ever spent.

On the day before they were due to leave, Elizabeth was walking in the shrubbery with Caroline while Rufus had taken Joseph for a drive. Sophie had been busying herself with some last-minute tasks when there was a knock on the drawing room door and a visitor was announced. Arthur, who had been her devoted servant almost since the moment he had first set foot in Rose Cottage, had no knowledge of the man who had presented himself at the door, and it was without foreboding that he announced, "Mr Follet to see you, Miss Clifford."

Creamy skin turned to porcelain, and she had to grip the back of a chair in order to steady herself. Was he come to brazen it out? He could not know, surely, that there was proof of his perfidy. Why was he here? Without the protection of Rufus or her father she suddenly became very fearful, but there was no sign of it as she drew on her courage and invited him to sit down. She remained standing. "I must say, Francis, that I am more than a little surprised to see you. How you came by my direction I do not know, but you must know you are not welcome here."

"Come now, Sophie, are we not brother and sister? I know we didn't part on good terms, but can we not let bygones be bygones?"

"You know as well as I that we are not brother and sister and no, too much has passed between us for me to forget. You have insulted me unforgivably and I am at a loss to know what you think to achieve by coming here today."

Follet lounged back in his chair, apparently at ease, and smirked at her, more condescending than ever. "I had heard that you had removed to the country. I can only imagine the distress you must have felt when you were shunned by Society, and I cannot blame you for your retreat. I have come, my dear, to rescue you. Only marriage can restore your good name. I trust you have now perceived your error in rejecting me and come once again to offer you my protection."

Sophie was consumed by a rage greater than any she had ever experienced. "You are mistaken, Francis. Society has not rejected me, something you would know if you had remained in London. My parentage is acknowledged and I am welcomed in places where you would not be able to set foot."

"Ah yes, your father. And how is he these days?"

She felt as though she was taking part in one of the farces she had seen at the theatre. Her manner became colder than ever and she said, "My father has been the subject of a dastardly attack. He was waylaid on Finchley Common when returning to town. He was shot and left for dead."

Follet managed to contrive an expression of sympathy and said, "I am so sorry, my dear. Please accept my sincerest condolences."

"You do not listen, Francis. I said *left* for dead," she said frostily, her anger overcoming any fear she might previously have felt. "But he did not die. Wait a moment, for there is something I would show you." She went to retrieve the button which had been placed in the bureau for safekeeping. "Perhaps you recognise this. I certainly did when first it was shown to me. My father plucked it from the coat of his attacker. It is one of a set I sewed for you. And you have the audacity to come here today with this on your conscience! Except that I doubt you have any conscience. My father lives, Francis, and can mark you for the man who attempted to murder him."

Suddenly he was on his feet and had thrust the chair aside. He grabbed her by the throat and she could see all at once how he might have committed such a foul deed. Never had she seen such hatred or anger in anyone's face and she thought it would be the last thing she ever saw, so certain was she that he was about to throttle her. And then she was released, and Follet lay at her feet on the floor and Rufus's arms were about her, his hand stroking her hair, his lips whispering words of comfort into her ear. "My dearest. My darling. Don't cry. I cannot bear it. That he should have laid a finger upon you, and I not here to protect you. You are safe now. Don't cry."

Templeton, who had followed Luxton into the room, walking now with the aid of a stick, watched this exchange with satisfaction before ringing for Arthur to bring some rope so they could tie the creature up before he might do any more damage. Not that he was likely to, for Rufus had knocked him out cold. However, it would give Joseph considerable gratification to have the cur at a disadvantage when he came to. Cross-examining him was a pleasure he was no longer prepared to forego. When the footman returned, he asked him to ensure that Lady Luxton and Miss Ward were kept away

194

from the drawing room by whatever ruse he could think of, it not being suitable for them to see what was going on.

"Miss Sophie, sir. Is she all right? I didn't know. I wouldn't have let him in but he seemed perfectly gentlemanlike." The man was practically in tears and Joseph sought to reassure him. "You could not have realised, Arthur. Do not distress yourself. Just go now and make sure you keep the ladies away."

"Yes, sir, of course, sir."

Sophie had by this time ceased sobbing and was sitting on the couch, a very bleak look in her eyes. Rufus hauled the inanimate body from the floor and onto a chair where his hands and feet were secured. Purely for dramatic effect, they placed him opposite the couch and sat on each side of Sophie, facing him as though he were a prisoner in the dock. He groaned and they knew he was coming round. As he opened his eyes with difficulty, for Rufus had broken his nose and all his urbanity had fled, Joseph opened the proceedings.

"Good day, Follet. What a pleasant surprise. I must say, I hadn't thought to see you again."

Follet spat some blood from his mouth and hatred flamed in his eyes. He spoke with difficulty. "You should be dead. Why aren't you dead?" He seemed bewildered.

"It would seem you made a hash of it, just as you have made a hash of everything else. But I'm curious to know. Why were you so desirous of putting paid to my existence?"

"It was nothing personal. You were merely the means to an end."

It took Templeton only a moment to digest this statement before he said incredulously, "You sought to wreak your revenge on my daughter by killing me? What sort of a man are you?"

Sophie had stiffened, but she was restrained by the pressure of Rufus's hand and sat back once more.

"You cannot know. I was but a toddler when my mother married Clifford. All my life he has led me to believe that one day Sophie would be my wife. That her riches would be mine. She had no idea that she stood to inherit untold wealth," he said, pausing only to sneer at her. "The baron kept her close and I was in a fair way to persuading her to marry me until that day she was thrown from her horse." Sophie could not believe he could have been so deluded when she had rejected him so many times. "Then you took her in, Luxton. How I have despised you ever since. Showing her all those things which my stepfather had been so careful to keep from her. Making her believe there was another world outside of Charnwood. And I, who surely had more right than anyone, was countered at every turn. You thought I didn't know I'd been deliberately excluded from the guest list for Miss Solgrave's ball. I managed to foil you that time, didn't I? What else could you do but invite me to attend?"

Sophie stared at him in astonishment. Surely he was mad!

He was continuing, turning his face now from Rufus to her. "Once more you spurned me. Looked down upon me as if I wasn't worthy of your notice. I had an ace up my sleeve, though. I knew about your father. Knew I could bring about your social downfall. That you would have to accept me, for no other would offer for you when the truth came to light."

"Do you hate me so much?"

There was steel in his eyes as he said, "Oh yes. So much of my childhood was centred upon you, you see. And then you wouldn't have me. I had been promised the moon and was given only the dirt beneath your feet. Of course I hate you."

There was silence as his words hung in the air. And there was no doubt in the minds of the three observers that at some point Follet had gone over the edge of sanity into madness. Templeton once more took charge of the conversation.

"You are aware that I have evidence to send you to prison for the rest of your life? I would prefer that no more scandal attach itself to my daughter and am therefore prepared not to prosecute you. Let it be understood, though, that you are to leave these shores and, should I ever learn that you have once more set foot in England, I shall bring all the power of justice to bear down upon you. Do I make myself understood?"

Follet merely nodded, broken now that he had divested himself of his vitriol.

"And do you agree?"

Another nod. "What else can I do?"

"Then I shall see to it that you are escorted to the coast and placed upon a ship bound for the Americas. You may think yourself lucky that I have not killed you with my bare hands, for a more evil person I have never met before today."

He rang the bell and asked Arthur to send for John Drummond. "John, you will oblige me by taking this creature away and confining him in the stables until such time as I can organise his removal. Do not give him any quarter. He is to remain tied up and a guard placed at his door."

Drummond left with his prisoner in tow and a strange silence fell upon the room. Sophie was the first to break it.

"I have gone from anger to disbelief to an overwhelming sadness. How can such a man exist?"

"Greed will do much to people, my darling," said Rufus, "and you heard him say, he was filled with expectations from a child. They have turned his mind so he was unable to contemplate anything else. Joseph, I commend you on your decision and with your permission I will contact one of my army friends. I make no doubt he will know exactly how to deal with just such a situation."

Templeton was showing signs of exhaustion and said he would be grateful now to have the matter taken out of his hands. He took himself off to bed, leaving Sophie and Rufus to recover as best they could.

She stepped into his arms. It seemed to be the most natural place in the world to her and the trembling which had racked her body slowly subsided. By the time Elizabeth and Caroline entered the room some twenty minutes later she was calm again and they were able, she and Rufus, to explain what had occurred. Had she been allowed, Lady Luxton would have marched straight to the stables and given Follet a piece of her mind, but she caught her son's eye over Sophie's shoulder and the message he sent her was clear enough. Instead she declared she still had much to do if they were to depart the next day as planned.

"I will leave Drummond here, and Wilfred too, until such time as the arrangements for that contemptible scoundrel are complete, Mama. I see no reason why we should delay our departure. After all, we have a wedding to plan," he added, trying to ease the tension.

"I have loved my time here at Rose Cottage, but now I cannot wait to abandon it. Francis has tainted so much of my life, but I shall not permit him to do so anymore. Tomorrow we shall all of us go home." Sophie had never before referred to Ashby as home, but even as she did so she reflected upon her time there in those early days when Elizabeth had taken her in and nurtured her. She realised now that she did indeed regard it as home. She said, striving for a conversational tone, "May I have a dog, Rufus? I was never permitted to have a dog before. The baroness maintained they brought her out in a rash and must be confined below stairs. She never did understand that I wanted something of my own to love."

"You may have as many dogs as you desire and they may roam the house at will, if that's what it takes to make you happy."

She looked shyly at him but replied with complete sincerity, "No, my love, I do not require a dog to make me happy. It is you who does that for me." And then the impish smile that so delighted him returned. "But there's no denying it would help."

CHAPTER TWENTY-TWO

Rufus and Sophie chose to ride the distance between Rose Cottage and Ashby. She left without a backward glance, desirous only of putting as much distance as possible between her and her loathsome stepbrother. Earlier in the day Elizabeth had taken Joseph Templeton up in her carriage and set forth in good order with another following, piled high with Sophie and Luxton's belongings, and a third carrying two abigails and a happy Arthur. The young footman had appeared almost overcome when informed by his mistress that he was to accompany her, sure as he had been that he would have to find new employment.

"You have shown yourself to have my interests at heart, Arthur. I am sure a place can be found for you at Ashby, should you wish to come."

Bursting with pride, he couldn't wait to tell his ma and pa. In the meantime, he sat chatting happily with Bertha, all the while under the watchful but benevolent eye of Lady Luxton's maid. Meanwhile, Caroline Ward accompanied Rufus and Sophie, grateful for the opportunity to ride. It was an activity she expected to have to forego in the future, Elizabeth not participating in the sport. But Sophie said, after they had slowed from a canter to a walk, "I am hoping we will continue to ride together at Ashby, Caroline. The dower house is not so far from the main house that we shouldn't comfortably be able to do so."

"I need not tell you, I am sure, how happy that would make me. If Lady Luxton can spare me, I should like nothing better."

"My mother was an active horsewoman in her younger days, Miss Ward. She no longer rides but would be the first, I am certain, to encourage you to participate in a pastime she has herself previously so much enjoyed."

It seemed that everyone was facing a bright future. The riders had overtaken the carriages long before their destination was reached. As they passed the oak tree where Sophie's accident had occurred, she couldn't help but reflect that, all things considered, life had been very good to her.

She was touched to find a welcoming party awaiting her, the staff lined up to greet her as she entered the house. She could not judge whether it had been Rufus or his mother, or indeed the housekeeper, who had arranged such a reception, but nothing was more certain than that all were aware that they were receiving their new mistress. As for Sophie, though she maintained an outward appearance of calm, inwardly her heart was full and only the warm glance she bestowed upon her betrothed gave any indication of how affected she was by the gesture. She spoke to each person in turn, even those she had previously not met, thus winning the instant allegiance of all. Elizabeth had not yet moved into the dower house. She wouldn't do so until the wedding, and Sophie and Rufus sat in happy contentment to await the arrival of the cavalcade, Caroline having retired to her room.

"Well, my bride, I trust your homecoming was as you would have wished."

"Was it you who arranged it? Such a wonderful gesture."

"Far be it from me to steal another's thunder. It was my mother who sent word ahead that it should be so. She is fonder of you than you could know, Sophie."

"Then I am content, for so I am of her, though why she should feel thus I cannot tell."

"And that in itself is one of the reasons. Tell me where you would like to go on your honeymoon. The world is your oyster."

Sophie placed a thumb beneath her chin as if contemplating and then laughed, the deep gurgle that gave him so much delight. "I should like to go to Rome, I think, and to Florence, and to Paris. But not immediately. We have journeyed, have we not, from pillar to post these last few months? I would prefer to remain at Ashby for a while, if you have no objection. Only think, Rufus, it will all be vastly strange to Elizabeth, moving from here to the dower house. I know she will have Caroline to bear her company, but I have no doubt a settling-in period will be required. Let us put off travelling while she accustoms herself."

He swept her from her chair and into his arms and left her gasping for breath as the sound of horses announced the arrival of the carriages. When Elizabeth and Joseph entered the room a few moments later Sophie was seated, apparently composed, in a wing chair, and Rufus was staring intently out of the window to the garden beyond.

"I am hoping that you have advised Cook that we have with us one of huge appetite. Joseph has been speaking of nothing but his supper for the last hour, and I must admit to feeling a little peckish myself."

"No such thing, Mama," he said, tearing his gaze from whatever he was pretending to focus on to answer her. "Sophie and I have already taken a light meal. I was certain you would have broken your journey and have ordered nothing."

Only for a moment did Elizabeth hesitate before breaking into laughter and accusing her son of being a tease. "I shall go and change immediately. See if you cannot bring supper forward before I faint from hunger." She left the room, still chuckling.

It was while they were eating that Rufus announced his intention of riding over to Charnwood the next morning.

"When there is so much to do here?" his mother questioned.

"I know, but think if you will. I don't know if Follet was expected home yesterday, but Clifford must be informed of his departure without delay. It may be that he wishes to take his leave of him, and I for one am of the opinion he should not be denied the opportunity. We cannot know if the baron was aware of his stepson's activities. For myself, I would doubt it. Even less so the baroness, and to remove her son willy-nilly would be cruel in the extreme."

There was a moment's silence as his words sank in before Elizabeth replied, "I hadn't considered that aspect. As a mother, if there is any love between them I cannot imagine the anguish she will have to endure at the prospect of never seeing her child again."

"Would you wish me to go with you?" Sophie asked with a reluctance she was at pains to conceal.

"The choice must be yours, my darling, but try if you will to consider it from Clifford's point of view. I would judge that your presence could only exacerbate the situation for them. It might be best if you remain here at Ashby."

She could not but be grateful and understood his reasoning. "Then I shall send no message. I don't in any case know what to say, and I rely on you to convey on my behalf anything you think appropriate. I have no love for either of them, but I wouldn't wish such a situation upon anybody and can only feel deeply sad for them."

Rufus looked at Joseph, who had remained quiet thus far. "Do you have anything you wish to add, sir?"

"I have not. I can find no fault with your judgement and would only wish this frightful business over and done with. The Cliffords have blighted not just my life but that of my beautiful Harriet and my daughter also. The sooner we are done with them the better. That does not preclude me feeling the utmost sorrow for the position in which they will find themselves once you have imparted the news."

All were subdued and none wished to be sociable after they removed from the dining room. It had been a tiring day, and after travelling from Cholesbury to Ashby everyone chose to retire early. Sophie joined Rufus on the terrace where he was having a quiet smoke before going to bed.

"So much of my trouble has fallen upon your shoulders. When I think of my life, had I not met you…"

"Then don't think of it. Soon we will be wed. We can put the past behind us and look forward to our shared future. Now kiss me before you go, for I will be up and off in the morning before your head has left the pillow."

It was a tender embrace that they shared. She left him standing there and went to dream of weddings and flowers. Somewhere in there was a small dog, and in her unconscious state Sophie smiled.

CHAPTER TWENTY-THREE

True to his word, Rufus was gone before anyone else had stirred. He reached Charnwood in good time and surprised his host, who had not yet sat down to breakfast. The earl received a cold reception initially until Clifford had time to wonder at the gravity of his expression and dismissed the servants, anxious to discover what had brought Luxton to see him. Calling for coffee to be brought to the study, he led his visitor there, gestured to a chair and said, "It would seem you come on an errand of some significance. Do not beat around the bush. What has occurred to bring you here so early in the day?"

Both men sat down and Rufus came straight to the point. "You may not be aware that your stepson made an attempt on Joseph Templeton's life some six weeks ago."

He was permitted to go no further. "What! How dare you come here making such an accusation?"

"I'm sorry. There can be no doubt. Templeton has irrefutable proof. The reason for my visit today is to inform you that he has chosen not to bring down the force of the law upon him. Instead he is to be transported to the Americas, never to return to England. Follet has agreed to these terms and is waiting even now for arrangements to be made to put him on a ship."

Clifford ran a hand through his hair and looked entirely bewildered. "You said this happened weeks ago. How is it that action is only now being taken?"

Rufus went on to explain Follet's visit to Cholesbury. "He told us he had all his life been led to believe that Miss Clifford would be his wife and that her fortune would become his. Though she had rejected him several times, he would not accept her answer, feeling that he had only to persist in order to change her mind. And then she removed from Charnwood and out of his reach. Still he pursued her, and when she would not have him he chose to wreak his revenge by taking her father's life." Rufus paused, allowing time for his words to sink in.

The baron looked stunned, and Luxton was in no doubt that all this was news to him. He seemed to shrink in on himself as the enormity of the situation struck home.

"How am I going to tell my wife? She will want to see him. Can we do so? You say he is still in the county. Would you permit us to go to him? How on earth am I going to tell my wife?" he repeated.

"I will escort you myself, sir, if that is your wish. I shall leave you now, for you will want to be alone with the baroness. If you do not send me a message later today, I will return in the morning to take you to him."

He stood, the coffee untouched beside him, and bowed his head, leaving the room as Clifford waved one hand in his direction, the other supporting his head, too bemused even to escort his visitor to the door. Outside once more, Rufus let out his breath and mounted his horse. Tomorrow would be an ordeal for all concerned, himself included, but today he would go home and spend the rest of the time with his family.

With no word from Clifford, Rufus set off early again the following morning. Both the baron and his wife were waiting and it was fortunate, Luxton thought, that the carriage made conversation difficult. He did not know what to say to them.

When they arrived at Rose Cottage, Wilfred ran from inside the stables to the horses' heads. His master jumped down and had a quick word with his tiger. He didn't want to further distress Follet's parents, but neither was he prepared to leave the man unrestrained. In the end he decided to have the ropes removed, but Drummond stood by the door to prevent any attempt at escape. All this he whispered to Wilfred before turning to aid the baroness down from his carriage.

By the time they had entered the building Francis was sitting quietly in his chair, unbound but with all the appearance of a broken man. Mother ran to son, her sobs a bar to any conversation. She embraced him while the baron looked on. He turned to Rufus and said, "I have brought some of his things in the small trunk which was loaded onto the back of your carriage. If you have no objection, I would appreciate it if he could be allowed to take them with him." He paused. "I am happy for you to examine everything. In your position I would want to do so myself." Luxton could only be grateful for the other man's common sense. The baron turned to his stepson, putting a hand on his wife's shoulder so that she drew back a little. "I am given to understand, Francis, that you have committed a foul deed and that there is proof of your perpetration. Do you have anything to say in your defence?"

Francis looked sulky and shrugged. "You always told me Sophie would be mine. I can tell you now she wouldn't have me. Ever since she left home she has been puffed up in her own esteem, and it seems I wasn't good enough for her. Little did she know that she was misbegotten."

Clifford flinched but answered, "It is my understanding that she was made aware of her parentage some months ago. Why now, after all this time, would you choose to act as you did?"

"I wanted to hurt her."

It was simply said but the anguish it engendered in his mother was painful to observe. She wailed and rocked herself back and forth. Her husband appeared to be turned to stone. Rufus reached out and touched his elbow, but he was shaken off and the baron spoke once more.

"What you have done is unspeakable. You may count yourself lucky that it was not I in whose hands lay your punishment. I should not have been so lenient. I will wait outside, for I can no longer bear the sight of you. Say your goodbyes to your mother and may God forgive you, for I never shall." With that he turned on his heel and left the room. Rufus also removed himself, compassionate enough to give the two these last few minutes alone.

Clifford, looking every bit as defeated as his stepson, said, "I think that, upon reflection, I shall be brought to realise that some blame must be laid at my door. Sadly much of what Francis said is true, but I never thought he would take my wishes as fact or bring matters to such an extreme. My only request, for he deserves no quarter, is that you ensure that his passage may be as smooth as possible. He has been indulged all his life. For his mother's sake I would wish that he might arrive safely at his destination. After that..." He shrugged. "After that, it is to be hoped he can recognise the opportunity he has been given and will make something of his life. I will step outside to take some air while we wait for my wife. I will not speak of this again, Luxton, but I thank you for your handling of such a sensitive situation." Rufus forbore to mention that it was Templeton to whom he owed his thanks.

Feeling he had done as much as he could, Rufus returned to Ashby, by which time the day was much advanced. Sophie and his mother were waiting anxiously for news. He outlined in detail what had happened and Sophie, perhaps for the first time in her life, found herself in sympathy with the baron and, more especially, her stepmother.

"I think Clifford was shocked beyond belief," said Rufus. "Perhaps he had never before considered how strongly he had wished for a union between you and his stepson and how impressionable Follet was. Who knows, perhaps a move across the ocean will be the making of him. It is my understanding that there are many opportunities in the New World. I have written to Freddie Conroy. As well as being a friend from my army days he is also my brother-in-law, and I thought it best to keep things in the family. I have the utmost confidence in his ability to shut down this whole business for us."

"The Earl of Luxton rides once more to the rescue," Sophie said in admiration.

"Well, I for one have much to be grateful to you for," said Templeton. "And I should be even more grateful if you would take me for a drive tomorrow. I have been a prisoner of these two women for twenty-four hours, and they can talk of nothing else but your forthcoming wedding. What would you, Luxton? I am a mere man and, not yet being fit to ride or to walk any great distance, I have been a captive audience. Only grant me some respite, if you will."

All four laughed and Rufus said he would be delighted, as it would be a means for him also to escape such discussions.

"It's easy for you to laugh, but there is much to be done," said Elizabeth. "In any event, there will be no such conversations tomorrow. I am taking Sophie over to the dower house. She will not be satisfied it will do for me until she has seen it herself."

"I should still like to go for a drive if you will oblige me, Luxton," said Templeton. "It does not suit me to be sitting day after day in one place."

"I fear you will not long remain at Ashby after the wedding, Papa," Sophie said, smiling but with a tinge of sadness in her voice.

"You are right, but doubtless you will soon grow tired of me for it is my intention to return often. I cannot go anywhere, of course, until John Drummond is restored to me. Tell me, my boy, how you found him at Rose Cottage."

Rufus laughed. "Champing at the bit and as eager as you to be on the move once more. You have a good friend there, Templeton."

"The best. I have become indebted to him over time, but never more so than now when I owe him my life."

"How did you come across him?"

"Ex-army. He was sitting in an inn in Paris, staring down at his glass as if the world had come to an end, and to all intents and purposes his had. I asked if I might join him. With the war over, he had been without occupation for a while and his life had no structure. By the end of the evening we had decided to join forces and have been together these past three years. I don't know what I'd do without him now."

"Should I then have asked him to deal with Follet?"

"No. He is a man who takes orders well, but would not relish the responsibility of putting such a plan in place. I feel sure you have done the right thing."

"Then we will discuss it no further. If you will excuse me, I will go outside to indulge myself in what my mother considers an abominable habit."

"It is no more odious than taking snuff, Rufus. I shall bid you goodnight and see you all again at breakfast."

Templeton too retired and Sophie, as if at some unspoken signal, joined Rufus on the terrace to sit in quiet contemplation.

CHAPTER TWENTY-FOUR

Sophie began the next day by writing to the Munros and hoped she had given them sufficient time to complete their arrangements.

My dearest grandparents,

All is marching on apace and a date for the wedding has been fixed two weeks hence. I would ask upon receipt of this letter that you set out as soon as you can from Yorkshire. It will, I trust, enable you to recover from the exertions of the journey and enter with us into the final family days before the 'big event'. Lydia (Luxton's sister) and her husband are to join us as soon as possible and are looking forward to meeting you. My father met with an accident which explains why there has been a delay, but he is now much recovered. He sends his best wishes to you both.

It is my earnest wish, and that of Rufus too, that you remain with us for a few weeks after the marriage has taken place. We are not presently planning a honeymoon. Buckinghamshire is beautiful at this time of year and we see no reason to pack our trunks and leave in haste. It would give us much pleasure to spend an extended period with you. Grandpapa, you may smile to learn that my husband-to-be has become much interested in the raising of sheep and the textile industry. I put this entirely at your feet. He could talk of little else following our inspection of the mill and his own journey to his estate nearby. He is hoping you will lend him your ear and give him some instruction, and I suspect it will not be long before you find us paying you another visit.

You cannot know how much I am looking forward to seeing you both again.

With fondest wishes,
Sophie

She went in search of Rufus to ask him to frank her letter, sharing the contents with him before he did so.

"What a kind soul you are, my dearest. Your grandparents would be less than human if they did not anticipate the coming weeks with some trepidation, taking into account all that has gone before. You have, in my opinion, done an admirable job of laying their fears to rest. You needn't think, either, that I do not notice you have committed me to paying more attention to my Yorkshire estate. Edward Boyle at least will be satisfied," he said with a laugh.

The dower house was built in the Tudor style and was an imposing structure, pleasing to the eye as one approached via the drive that wound between an ornamental garden to one side, graced with three statuettes, and a knot garden to the other. Sophie could feel Elizabeth's excitement as they drew near, and any doubts she may have had about evicting the countess from her home were laid to rest before they had even crossed the threshold.

"Is it not beautiful, Sophie? I cannot wait to show you what I have achieved. It has been many years since anything was done here and it has undergone a complete refurbishment."

Sophie looked around her as they entered the hall. An imposing oak staircase was shown to advantage by the sunlight cast upon it through a huge bay window which ran from floor to ceiling. What might have been a dark area because of its many wooden beams was thrown into relief by the whitewash between them and a marble floor, evidently a late addition, added light to the whole.

"It is delightful. If this is an example of what is to come, I can see why you are so pleased with it."

The two women spent the rest of the morning examining the building from top to bottom. Elizabeth had put a fine touch onto all, and what had once been a dingy house was being turned into a bright and welcoming home.

"I shall certainly know where to come when your son is away from Ashby. I never saw a more sociable house."

"And you will always be welcome. The garden too suits me admirably. It isn't too large and is separated from the rest of the estate by a high hedge, which grants me all the privacy I might wish."

By the time everything had been inspected and the two ladies were back in the main house, Luxton and Templeton had returned from their drive. So lovely was the weather that they all took a light lunch together on the terrace and Sophie was able to tell Rufus that her fears had now been laid to rest. "Your mother has a keen eye and everything has been done to perfection."

"I trust you are not planning to turn Ashby upside down as well," he said, earning the gurgling response he loved so much.

"Oh no, not yet anyway."

Freddie Conroy, having wasted no time, arrived with Lydia the following day. Pausing only long enough to settle his wife into her former home, he set off for Rose Cottage, anxious to fulfil his mission and return to Ashby.

"You do me a great favour, Freddie," Rufus said, shaking his friend's hand as Conroy, mounted on a borrowed horse, prepared to leave. "I just ask that you beware. Follet is a devious man and, I think, a little deranged. Do not give him any quarter. But John Drummond will know. I will look for you within the week."

"Think nothing of it, old boy. From what you tell me, this country will be well rid of such a blackguard. I shall know just how to deal with him. Take care of your sister for me."

When Rufus returned to the house there was no sign of the women and he persuaded Templeton to a game of billiards. In the meantime, Elizabeth had borne her daughter off to her old bedchamber. Dismissing Lydia's maid, the countess reclined on the chaise longue while Sophie and Lydia perched on the edge of the bed. Caroline, who had been invited to join them, had declined, saying she had a letter to write home, but in truth she was being discreet, judging it best to leave the family alone.

"What a perfect companion she is, Sophie. She seems to have an instinct for knowing when her presence is required and when it is best for her to retire. Now tell me everything, Lydia. It seems an age since I last saw you."

"Well, Mama, there is little to tell. I find married life suits me admirably. Freddie's parents are a delight and have welcomed me with a warmth I could not have anticipated. His mother tells me how overjoyed she is that he has settled down, for he seemed to have lost purpose after leaving the army."

"I am delighted you are so well established. Are you in the habit of entertaining? I assume your husband must have a large acquaintance in the area."

Lydia looked at her mother and then at Sophie. Her eyes were sparkling and a smile played around her mouth. "At first we did, but not so much of late. Freddie doesn't want me to exert myself, you see."

It didn't take a huge intellect to understand what she was telling them and Elizabeth jumped up to embrace her daughter while Sophie expressed her delight by squeezing her hand.

"It is not obvious yet, and we haven't told his parents as I wished to share the news with you first, Mama. I have been quite well, having suffered only slight nausea in the first few weeks. While I am here I would like to find my old christening robe, for I should dearly like my own babe to wear it when the time comes."

"Finding it will not be a problem. I have a trunk full of your childhood clothes and toys." A misty look flickered across Elizabeth's features. "I shall have it brought here immediately. What fun we will have examining the contents."

Lydia assured her that the next day would be soon enough. "I am certain it will not be an exercise of merely a few moments. I would prefer to return to the drawing room now to see my brother. I would like to tell him he is to become an uncle. And your father, Sophie? How is he? Is he returned to full health, do you think?"

"Very nearly so, I believe. I think he will not long remain here after the wedding. Before then we also have a hurdle to cross when my grandparents arrive at Ashby. My feeling, though, is that all the parties involved will be at pains to put the past behind them. I am confident of a happy outcome."

Rufus, when advised of his sister's condition, picked her up and twirled her around the room in delight before depositing her very gently back on her feet.

"May I add my congratulations to those of everyone else, Mrs Conroy, and may I be permitted to say your condition suits you," said Joseph. "You are positively blooming."

"Thank you, and I should much prefer it if you would call me Lydia."

"Of course, just as long as you agree to call me Joseph."

James and Nancy Munro reached Ashby before Freddie had returned from his mission. They arrived mid-afternoon and Sophie and Rufus ran down the steps to greet them.

"Well, boy, it's a fine-looking place you have here, though not as large as Munro Manor. But you have the history, son. I'll give you that. Help my lady down if you would," James said, turning to embrace his granddaughter before standing back to look at her face. "We're not much given to expansive compliments in Yorkshire, but I'll say this, lass. You're a sight for sore eyes. Here's your grandmother now."

Sophie hugged Nancy, wanting to put her at ease. "I hope you are not too tired out by the journey, Grandmamma. I cannot tell you how much I appreciate you coming all this way."

"Tired out! What do you take me for when I had nowt to do but sit all day? I should be grateful for the opportunity to stretch my legs, but first I would like to go inside and meet Lady Luxton. And your father, of course."

Her husband took her elbow and they entered the hall just as Elizabeth ran to meet them.

"You cannot know how pleased I am to see you. Sophie has talked so much of you both that I feel I know you already. But come into the drawing room. The footman will take your hat," she said, drawing Nancy's arm through her own. As they entered, Joseph Templeton rose from his chair and Elizabeth felt the tension run through Nancy's arm into hers. As forceful a personality as her husband, though, she moved away from her hostess to greet him.

"You will first allow me have my say, if you please," she began, holding up her hand as he stepped forward. "It has been many years since we last met and nearly as many that I have been unable to acquit myself of blame for what followed.

I make no excuses, for there are none. None that would be acceptable, in any case, either to you or to me and my husband. Or … or to Harriet, were she alive today. Could we but turn back time. However, we cannot, and while our actions are beyond forgiveness, and therefore we do not ask it of you, we would beg that you will allow us into the present, that we may share the joy that is your daughter and our granddaughter."

"I am not without sin," Templeton replied. "Once Harriet was married, I should have walked away. I did not have the strength to do so. And recently I have had reason to be grateful that I did not. We have all of us lost someone who was precious beyond words, but we have what she left to us in Sophie. If you will permit, I should count it a privilege to embrace you all as family."

There. It was said. For once James Munro had maintained silence in a situation that was potentially filled with friction. No-one seemed to know what to say next until Sophie broke the tension. "Come, Grandmamma. For all your protestations, I think you would do well to sit down. Rufus, perhaps you could arrange for some refreshment. Lydia, may I make known to you Mr and Mrs Munro. Grandpapa, Mrs Conroy is the earl's sister. Her husband is away at present but will join us in a day or so."

As people took their places, Rufus had an opportunity to whisper in her ear before he left the room. "I knew you would make an admirable countess. Bravo."

Before long, conversation was flowing quite naturally. James Munro made reference to Templeton's accident and expressed the hope that he was quite recovered. Joseph, knowing they had not been made aware of the circumstances, merely asserted that he had a constitution of iron and had put all that behind him.

Once the Munros' rooms had been made ready they permitted themselves to be escorted away to rest, and Sophie turned to her father.

"Are you all right, Papa? I imagine that must have been quite an ordeal for you."

He smiled kindly upon her. "I saw only two elderly anxious people. It was not for me to rake over coals that have long grown cold. Whatever your situation might have been when you were at Charnwood, you now have a loving family who want only the best for you."

The following day Sophie spent a quiet morning with Nancy and James. They talked mostly of Harriet: how she'd follow her father's coattails as he went about his business; her childish intention to raise her own sheep; her intrepidity as a horsewoman, something their granddaughter told them she had inherited.

"She weren't one to stick to her books or her sewing. Often thought she ought to have been a boy, tha knows."

"But then she changed, didn't she, James? One day she was a scrubby child and then, overnight it seemed to me, she turned into a beautiful young woman. Not that she cared about that. Not until she fell for young Templeton. Your grandfather and I, we didn't recognise it for what it was. He was her first, you see. Not for a moment did we think it would last. Well, we've had plenty of time since then to realise how wrong we were."

"Don't distress yourself, Grandmamma. You did what you thought was best for your daughter. Now dry your tears and allow me to take you to my bedchamber and show you my wedding gown. No, not you, Grandpapa. This is women's work, but I understand you are partial to a game of billiards. I shall see if I cannot find Rufus to give you a game."

In the end it was Joseph who indulged the old man, and in spite of the history between them they got on pretty well. By mid-afternoon, the Munros were forced to admit that all this jaunting about the country had taken its toll and perhaps an hour or two's rest might be best. "And I'll get my revenge later, young man. After dinner, do you hear me, Templeton? I'll allow you this. You play a skilful game."

It seemed that the two were on the way to establishing an understanding, and nothing could have pleased Sophie more.

CHAPTER TWENTY-FIVE

By lunchtime the following day, Conroy and Drummond had returned to Ashby and were able to report that Follet had embarked on the ship that was to carry him away. There was a joyful reunion between Freddie and Lydia following what had been their longest separation since their marriage, and Joseph carried Drummond off to a nearby alehouse to catch up on recent events.

Sophie was sitting in the garden with Rufus and her grandparents when she looked up to see Arthur escorting a visitor towards them. The man stopped and it was clear he was considering retreating, so obvious was the half turn he made before resuming his approach. She had only time to say in an undertone, "The baron is here," before he joined them. Rufus stood up to greet him. The Munros appeared to be turned to stone.

"Good day, Luxton. Sophie. Mr and Mrs Munro. I would not have invaded your privacy had I known, but now that I'm here I hope you will allow me to remain for long enough to fulfil my errand."

No-one replied and he took their silence for assent, lowering himself onto the bench indicated by Rufus. The stillness extended for some moments, becoming embarrassingly uncomfortable. Rufus filled the gap by asking, "You come on an errand, you say?"

Clifford seemed to pull himself together and, turning to the older couple, said, "I do. But first I would address you." It looked as if Munro was about to protest, but he continued. "No, please hear me out. I did not expect to find you here and

I would not have come, had I known. I have lately been brought to understand that my actions have caused repercussions of which I could not have dreamed. Those actions began with my rejection of you and the separation firstly from your daughter and latterly your grandchild. Arrogance and ambition both played their part, but that wasn't sufficient for me," he said bitterly. "I continued to isolate Sophie and, perhaps worst of all, did not inform her that she had living grandparents. She was a malleable child, her independent nature not showing itself until much later, and she asked no questions in that regard. In addition, I led my stepson to believe that one day they would marry and he would inherit a fortune. Your fortune, Munro. It is only recently that I have learned that money cannot buy happiness."

Clifford stopped and mopped his brow and nobody rushed in to fill the gap. They waited until he composed himself again. "It seems I placed too much emphasis on my ambition, which in turn became Francis's ambition. I had no idea how deeply it ran until a short while ago when Luxton informed me that my stepson had attempted to put a period to Templeton's life. It seemed that Sophie's rejection caused him to seek revenge by eliminating her newfound happiness."

He paused again, for it was evident from the countenance of each that neither Munro knew of these events. Still they did not speak, but their eyes never left his face.

"This brings me to my errand. After Sophie left Charnwood, I brought Harriet's jewellery box to her. You will remember it, I am sure, since you gave it to her yourself." He turned now to Sophie. "Since the banishment of your stepbrother, I have been going through his possessions, something too upsetting for his mother to do herself. I found this." He pulled a small case from his pocket and handed it to her "The box had always been left in my wife's care. I can only suppose Francis had access to it when he visited her in her bedchamber and found an opportunity to secrete it. Open it, for it is yours."

Inside was a string of pearls, doubtless those her grandfather had alluded to when she had carried the box to Yorkshire. She picked up the necklace and caressed it lovingly.

"I know not what he planned to do with it. I am at a loss to understand the workings of his mind. Sophie, you believed with justification that I behaved towards you throughout your life with a coldness not befitting a father. You may now be able to understand that my emotions were in conflict. So strong was my resentment of your real father that I was unable to demonstrate any affection towards you. I would like you to know, for I am aware this may be my last opportunity to tell you, that I have an abiding fondness for you which I will carry with me, even if I am never to see you again. I shall take my leave of you now, but believe me when I say that I wish you only happiness."

He left without another word. Nobody moved to prevent him.

Sophie sat in shocked silence. This man whom she had known all her life, whom she had feared all her life, had shown a side she'd never seen. Memories of her childhood flashed before her — times when she'd thought he was being cruel, but she could now see he'd been trying to protect her in his gruff way. Mostly it had been to do with horses. He had no empathy with them and couldn't understand how she might walk behind a mare's back legs without any apprehension. So he had shouted at her, and she had taken it for a reprimand. But he had cared.

She looked at Nancy and found she was being observed, that the same feeling of incredulity was reflected in her face. He whom they had all feared was himself afraid. Compassion rose within her and she almost ran after him, but too much had happened to go back. Instead, she moved to hug Nancy.

"He is to be pitied, Sophie, but he can damage us no longer. If you choose to do so, you can honour him, and us, and your mother by wearing her pearls at your wedding. What do you think?"

Sophie laughed. It was tremulous, but it was a laugh. "I think there is much still left that you can teach me, Grandmamma."

Neither Rufus nor James said anything. Seemingly sometimes men did know when it was best to keep silent.

CHAPTER TWENTY-SIX

The next few days were a flurry of activity. There were dress fittings to be undergone and hours when Sophie sat patiently while Bertha arranged her hair in a range of styles and Elizabeth, Lydia and Nancy all waited by to comment.

Lydia found that her slippers pinched. "No doubt because of your condition, my dear. Everything swells when one is expecting," said her mother. Rather than a trip to town, the shoemaker brought a selection to Ashby and naturally all four women found something that they had to have.

The ceremony was to take place in the small chapel which stood adjacent to the house. With thick stone walls and mullioned windows, it also boasted a small minstrels' gallery which faced the altar.

A few days before the wedding people had begun to arrive. Emily and Oliver, escorting the Dowager Lady Bridlington to Ashby, were the first guests to appear. No-one else came until the following day and the company split into well-defined groups. Luxton, his two army friends and Templeton formed one, all going off together to fish for trout. Elizabeth and Augusta greeted each other as though it had been years rather than weeks since they had last met. "You will be delighted, my dear Elizabeth, to learn that the awful Vaughan woman has finally received her just rewards, having spoken once too often to the wrong person in the wrong place. She and her husband are no longer received anywhere and Society is the better for it."

The morning of the wedding dawned bright and beautiful, and

Sophie sat up in bed as Bertha drew back the curtains.

"Just think, miss. By this time tomorrow you will be Sophie Solgrave, Countess of Luxton. Whoever would have thought it?"

Bertha was allowed the licence of a long-standing retainer and in any case the bride was in no mind to reprimand anyone, so happy was she. Bolstered by the pillows, Sophie sipped her hot chocolate and then jumped out of bed, eager to embrace what was to come. Bertha had brought a bowl of water and, as she splashed her face, Sophie looked out of the window. She had an unbroken view across the ornamental gardens where long shadows were thrown by a sun not yet riding high in the sky. Beyond were fields and the home wood where she had many times ridden Snowflake. She smiled, knowing that today her favourite would have to take exercise with another.

In no time it seemed her hair had been dressed with pearls and she was ready to step into her gown.

"Bixby, there is much that you do for me and I would be the first to acknowledge your talents, but one thing you must allow is for me to tie my own cravat," Rufus said to his valet at the same time as Sophie was donning her dress.

"Yes, my lord, of course." He looked wooden, but he had been with his master since his boyhood and Rufus wasn't deceived for one moment.

"I will try not to disgrace you, but this is one thing I must do for myself. Dammit, now I have ruined this one. Another, if you please."

"Very well, sir," Bixby said, handing Rufus a large square of white linen from the pile that was draped across his arm. "And if you stop talking, sir, you might be able to achieve the result you are after." His expression was unchanged, but Luxton had no doubt he was smiling inside.

For long seconds there was absolute silence. Rufus, whose head had been raised to the ceiling, slowly lowered his chin. At what was evidently a critical moment he turned it a fraction, first to the left and then to the right before once more bringing it down to a point above his chest. Lifting his head once more, he looked into the glass and said, "Yes, that will do."

Bixby laid the unused linen aside and picked up a midnight-blue fine cloth coat, holding it ready. It fitted as though moulded to the earl's muscular frame and he glanced once more into the mirror. His hair was brushed neatly into the Brutus style he always adopted. No crease marred the lines of his pantaloons. His boots gleamed with a shine that was the result of a secret application the valet would share with no-one. "Yes," Rufus repeated, "that will do."

An hour later Rufus was standing at the altar in the chapel talking quietly to the curate when a hush fell upon the assembled company. He turned his head to where the doors had been flung wide and Sophie entered on the arm of her father. Rufus's eyes never wavered from her face as she approached, and the room might have been empty of all but the two of them. Reaching the altar, Templeton gave his daughter's hand into that of her groom and together they moved to face the curate. He began the words that would change their lives forever. During the ceremony Sophie moved only once, when she raised her fingers to touch the pearls about her throat.

They removed to the house for the wedding breakfast, after which Rufus whispered in his wife's ear that her grandparents had asked if the bride and groom would join them in the drawing room. Worried there was something wrong, Sophie moved discreetly but swiftly.

"Don't be concerned, my love. They have assured me there is nothing amiss."

Waiting for them were only three people: Nancy and James Munro and her father.

"What is it?" Sophie asked anxiously.

"It is this," her grandfather said, going to the wall behind him and removing a cloth that covered the painting she had seen once before, when visiting Munro Manor. "Harriet would have liked you to have it, we are sure."

Sophie threw a swift look at her husband. "Did you know of this?"

He looked slightly ashamed but admitted he had been in on the secret. "It was necessary, when your grandparents arrived, to remove the portrait from their carriage without your knowledge. It was to be a surprise. A gift on your wedding day like no other."

She moved closer to examine her mother's features, knowing that in time she would become familiar with every single detail. Then she spoke to Nancy and James. "You could have given me nothing that would have meant more. And you, Papa, I make no doubt you too will draw comfort from seeing Harriet whenever you visit Ashby."

"And when I am not here, I have her locket," he answered, touching his breast where the treasure lay beneath his clothing. "Who could have dreamed of such a happy outcome?"

EPILOGUE

It was two weeks after the wedding. The guests had all gone. Elizabeth and Caroline had moved into the dower house and Sophie's father and John Drummond had left three days earlier, bound for foreign parts but with the promise to return before the turn of the year. Only Nancy and James Munro remained, and they were at present saying their goodbyes and boarding their carriage.

"We shall come and visit you in a few weeks, I promise," said Sophie. "Soon enough that we may return before winter sets in. Meanwhile, I shall write so often that my husband will doubtless refuse to frank my letters."

"If he keeps you short, you know where to come. Not that he's able to deny you anything from what I've seen, the two of you smelling of April and May as you do."

"Don't you worry, sir, I'll see she has everything her heart desires."

"Seems to me she has that already," Nancy said, trying to cover her emotion.

Sophie and Rufus stood waving until the coach was out of sight, and Sophie turned to go back into the house.

"Wait a moment if you would, my darling. I have reason to go to the stables and would ask you to walk with me."

"Allow me then to run inside and fetch some apples. Snowflake and the others will want to know what's wrong if we should arrive without a titbit for them."

She returned a few minutes later with a bag so full it could have fed every horse in the stalls and the loose boxes. Rufus relieved her of her burden and drew her arm through his free one.

"Will your errand take long, do you think?"

"No more than a few minutes. Are you anxious to be doing something else?"

"Oh no. It matters not what we do. It seems to be the first time we have been properly alone together since we were married." She blushed, realising the implication of what she had said. "No, I don't mean…"

"I know exactly what you mean and I feel it too. We have been surrounded by well-wishers and I think we could not have asked for more, but I cannot say I am sorry to have you to myself at last. Are you happy, Sophie? Will you miss having friends and family about you?"

She stopped walking and turned to face him, reaching up and putting her hands on either side of his face. She gave him to understand that she was perfectly content and could be happy with him on a desert island. After she'd had time to recover her breath, so emphatically had he kissed her, they continued on their way. When they reached their destination, she took an apple from the bag and ran ahead of him to greet Snowflake. Giving the rest of the apples to a groom who was standing by, she said, "I am ready now. Why are we here?"

"Your grandmother seems to believe you have everything your heart desires. Is that in fact so?" he said, looking so serious that she felt suddenly alarmed.

"Yes, you know I do. Is something wrong?"

"Are you sure there is nothing you wish for?"

"How can you ask me such a thing, Rufus? What is it? Tell me, please, for I am beginning to be afraid."

He set about reassuring her immediately, calling himself a cad for causing her any anxiety He took her hand and drew her with him to a stall at the far end of the building. "Open the door and go in."

She did so and there, curled up in the corner and sleeping peacefully, was a puppy. It couldn't have been more than eight weeks old, and she lifted it and held its tiny head to her cheek. "Rufus, he's beautiful. Thank you so very much."

"I seem to recall that you mentioned to me a while ago that you would like to have a dog. Did you not wonder why I had given you no gift upon our marriage? This little chap was not yet weaned, and I could not remove him from his mother. Come, bring him with you, for there is a blanket waiting for him in a corner of the scullery where he shall reside until such time as we decide what is to be the best place for him."

She looked up at him from under her lashes, a look of pure mischief covering her features. "Could we not perhaps place a box in the corner of our bedchamber?"

"No, Sophie, we could not!"

And they laughed, and were laughing still as they entered the house.

A NOTE TO THE READER

Dear Reader

I hope you have enjoyed reading *The Girl With Flaming Hair* as much as I enjoyed writing it.

A little escapism never did anyone any harm, and I spend much of my time in a world two hundred years in the past. The solace and pleasure and yes, deep joy, I take in the Regency era, both the reading and the writing of it, have multiplied as I've followed the adventures of heroes and heroines, created my own and woven stories around them, and laughed at the amazing wit of other authors. Somehow it all becomes so much more alive in the language of the early nineteenth century. For me there's a poetry about it, and I'm not talking iambic pentameter.

Sophie Clifford has been a much-loved figure for me but no more so than the lead characters to come in my next two books. I hope you will look out for them. Meanwhile stay safe and I look forward to seeing you next time.

If you would consider leaving a review on **Amazon** or **Goodreads**, it would be much appreciated, though I would be just as happy if you'd like to join me on my **Facebook author page** for a chat. You can also visit me on **Twitter**, **Instagram** and my **website**.

Natalie

nataliekleinman.com

Sapere Books is an exciting new publisher of brilliant fiction and popular history.

To find out more about our latest releases and our monthly bargain books visit our website:
saperebooks.com

Printed in Great Britain
by Amazon